Caught In The Act

Caught In The Act

Joan Lowery Nixon

BANTAM BOOKS
NEW YORK · TORONTO · LONDON · SYDNEY · AUCKLAND

CAUGHT IN THE ACT
A Bantam Book / April 1988

The Starfire logo is a registered trademark of Bantam Books.
Registered in U.S. Patent and Trademark Office and elsewhere.

Produced by Daniel Weiss Associates, Inc.,
27 West 20 Street, New York, NY 10011.

Library of Congress Cataloging-in-Publication Data

Nixon, Joan Lowery.
  Caught in the act / Joan Lowery Nixon.
    p.   cm.
  Summary: Eleven-year-old Michael Patrick Kelly from New York City
is sent to a foster home, a Missouri farm with a sadistic owner, a
bullying son, and a number of secrets, one of which may be murder.
  ISBN 0-553-05443-0
  [1. Foster home care—Fiction. 2. Missouri—Fiction. 3. Farm
life—Fiction.]   I. Title.
PZ7.N65Cau 1988
[Fic]—dc19

                                     87-30844
                                       CIP
                                       AC

Published simultaneously in the United States and Canada

Bantam Books are published by Bantam Books, a division of Bantam Doubleday
Dell Publishing Group, Inc. Its trademark, consisting of the words "Bantam Books"
and the portrayal of a rooster, is Registered in U.S. Patent and Trademark Office
and in other countries. Marca Registrada. Bantam Books, 666 Fifth Avenue,
New York, New York 10103.

PRINTED IN THE UNITED STATES OF AMERICA

FG   0 9 8 7 6 5 4 3

A Note From the Author

During the years from 1854 to 1929, the Children's Aid Society, founded by Charles Loring Brace, sent more than 100,000 children on orphan trains from the slums of New York City to new homes in the West. This placing-out program was so successful that other groups, such as the New York Foundling Hospital, followed the example.

The Orphan Train Quartet was inspired by the true stories of these children; but the characters in the series, their adventures, and the dates of their arrival are entirely fictional. We chose St. Joseph, Missouri, between the years 1860 and 1880 as our setting in order to place our characters in one of the most exciting periods of American history. As for the historical figures who enter these stories—they very well could have been at the places described at the proper times to touch the lives of the children who came west on the orphan trains.

Joan Lowery Nixon

CHILDREN

Without Homes.

A number of the CHILDREN brought from NEW YORK are still without homes.

FRIENDS FROM THE COUNTRY PLEASE

CALL AND SEE THEM.

MERCHANTS, FARMERS

AND FRIENDS GENERALLY

Are requested to give publicity to the above

AND MUCH OBLIGE

H. FRIEDGEN, Agent.

1

JENNIFER COLLINS HURRIED to the screened-in porch of Grandma Briley's home. She dropped into a comfortable wicker chair next to Grandma's and picked up the journal which had been written so long ago by Frances Mary Kelly. Tucked inside was the photograph of the girl with the long, dark hair who might almost have been Jennifer herself, if the old-fashioned dress and hair twisted into a soft bun hadn't given her away. Jennifer took the picture out and studied it again.

It was hard to think of the young woman in the sepia-toned picture as her great-great-great grandmother. Grandma had told Jennifer and Jeff that Frances had been eighteen when this photograph was taken. "Only three years older than I am now," Jennifer murmured.

A noise behind her startled Jennifer. She turned to see her twelve-year-old brother Jeff appear in the doorway cautiously balancing three glasses and a frosted pitcher of lemonade on a tray. He handed them over to

1

Grandma with a sigh of relief before he dropped into the nearest chair.

"Grandma's going to tell us *Mike's* story now," Jennifer told him.

Jeff glanced impatiently toward the quiet garden and mumbled, "I bet *Mike* had a lot of adventures after he went out West with the orphan train. I bet he got to do all kinds of exciting stuff—all the things I would have done if I'd been there."

He leaned over the arm of his chair toward Grandma. "Did Mike get to be a cowboy? Did he ever fight renegade Indians? Or get into a shootout with outlaws?"

"Be quiet, Jeff," Jennifer said. "Grandma, you told us that Mike suspected the man who adopted him of committing a murder, and I want to know what really happened."

Grandma laughed as she held up her hand. "You're both getting ahead of the story. Just be patient, listen, and you'll know all I know. I'll read from the opening of Mary's journal before I begin Mike's story." Grandma took the journal from Jennifer, opened it, and began to read.

As long as I live I shall never forget the misery and fear on Mike's face as he sat on the platform in that little church in St. Joseph, facing the people who had come to see the children from the Orphan Train.

Mr. Crandon, who had been so shocked and angry when he found out that Mike had been a copper stealer back in New York City, was moving from group to group, leaning close to whisper. Each couple to whom he spoke would immediately dart a glance toward Mike, some of them frowning, some staring with suspicion.

I wanted to cry out, "Don't listen to Mr. Crandon! Mike is a good boy. He didn't mean to do wrong. He

2

was so desperate to help feed our family, he just didn't think." But I couldn't speak out against Mr. Crandon. He was a successful businessman, well thought of in St. Joe; and we were strangers, orphans brought here from New York in the hope that some kindhearted people would offer us homes.

There was nothing I could do.

I thought about U.S. Army Captain Joshua Taylor, whom we had met on the orphan train. He had liked Mike. He'd praised Mike for his bravery. Oh, why couldn't someone as fine as the Captain have offered Mike a home? My heart ached as I saw Mike chosen by the Friedrichs. Mr. Friedrich seemed harsh and humorless, and I suspected that his only reason for adopting an Orphan Train child was to have an unpaid hired hand.

I hugged Mike tightly as we parted, hating to let him go, terrified of what might be in store for him.

2

MICHAEL PATRICK KELLY sat by himself in the wagon bed
behind the Friedrich family, grabbing the side for support each time the wheels dropped in and out of the ruts
and gullies in the dirt road. The first time the wagon
lurched, Mike sprawled on his back with a yelp, and
Gunter Friedrich—squeezed on the front seat between
his parents—turned to look at him with a mocking laugh.

Mike hated to be the laughing stock, and he was
beginning to dislike Gunter heartily. The next time the
wagon bounced so hard that it slapped his backside,
Mike met Gunter's stare by puffing out his cheeks and
arching his back so that his stomach protruded. Gunter's eyes narrowed, and he whirled around to face forward. Mike settled back, hoping he wouldn't be bothered
by Gunter again on this trip.

He had wished for a loving family and—even though no
one would ever replace his best friend and brother
Danny—he'd imagined there'd be a boy close to his age

who'd become his chum. Mike sighed. No such luck with Gunter.

The Friedrichs were not the kind of family Mike had pictured when Mr. MacNair and Mrs. Banks had described the new lives the Orphan Train children would lead in the West.

Hans Friedrich was balding and heavy. Mike shuddered as he remembered his first sight of Mr. Friedrich. His rounded stomach bulging from underneath his vest, his jowls quivering, he pointed at Mike and demanded of Andrew MacNair, the scout who found towns that would take the children, "That boy. We want him."

Mrs. Friedrich's head bobbed up and down eagerly. Her nose was like a round button in her rosy face, and her eyes were clear and blue, crinkled at the edges by her shy smile. But she flinched as her husband growled at her, "It's your fault we are late, Irma. Because of you, we missed getting a bigger, stronger boy. This boy is only what? Nine? Ten?"

"Eleven!" Mike said, insulted at the guess and earnestly wishing he weren't so small for his age.

Mrs. Friedrich tugged her shawl more tightly around her shoulders and stammered, "Th-the boy needs only some good food to make him grow tall and strong. Why, in no time he'll be like—like Gunter." She patted her son's arm, but Gunter shook her hand away.

Mike glanced at Gunter. He knew immediately that he had no desire to be anything at all like Gunter, who was fat and pasty, with hair so blond it was almost white. Gunter's expression was sullen. Mike wondered if he ever smiled. His thick lips were twisted into a pout. At the mention of his name, he scowled at the floor, kicking at an invisible spot with the toe of one shoe.

Obviously trying to make amends, Mrs. Friedrich smiled and said, "How fine it will be to have another boy in the house. He will be like a brother to you, Gunter."

5

"Don't want a new brother!" Gunter mumbled. "Brothers only cause trouble."

"Now, now." Mrs. Friedrich smiled nervously. "Soon the two of you will be the best of friends."

"Oh, no, we won't," Gunter hissed, his voice so low that Mike wondered if he were the only one who had heard him.

As soon as Andrew left Mike and the Friedrichs to get acquainted, Mr. Friedrich folded his arms across his chest, frowned at Mike, and said in a stern, loud voice, "So. You were a pickpocket. A thief."

Mike cringed as people nearby turned to stare at him. "Well, yes, I was. But I promised my mother and myself that I would never steal again," he replied. "I hope you'll believe me."

"I believe you," Mr. Friedrich answered, "because if you steal again, you will be beaten. You won't like the beatings, so you won't steal." The corners of his mouth tilted upward smugly. "I know now how to handle boys like you."

"Oh!" Mrs. Friedrich gasped. As she shot a quick glance at her husband, Mike noticed a fearful look in her eyes.

Gunter snickered and grinned a wicked grin. Mike's face grew hot with embarrassment. He wished he could punch Gunter right in his puffy, round nose. He wondered how old Gunter was. Maybe thirteen? Fourteen? He was taller and much heavier than Mike. Mike quickly decided that punching Gunter might not be a very good idea. After all, Gunter was part of his new family. And Mike usually got along with everyone he met, so he was surprised at his immediate dislike of Gunter. He decided to try and control his bad first impression.

*　　*　　*

6

Now, as he sat in the wagon bed, Mike thought about the bullies he'd known and had run-ins with in New York City. He had never let one of them get the best of him, and there was no way he was going to let Gunter get him down.

He looked around the landscape as the wagon plodded on, and his good spirits began to return. Low, rolling hills, many of them scattered with stalks and remnants of crops, a few still thick with high grain, some fragrant with the earthy smell of newly turned soil, stretched out around him. Golden-leaved trees were interspersed with deep green pines, and behind a wooden-rail fence Mike spotted a neat, small garden bursting with tangled vines and pumpkins larger than those he'd seen in the city's greengrocers' stalls.

Until he had left New York City on the Orphan Train, Mike had never seen open country. He missed the bustle and action of the city streets, but he supposed this quiet land might have something to recommend it, too. He wished it offered more excitement for a boy his age. He wished he were sixteen instead of eleven, so he could ride for the pony express. Galloping his horse through heat and snow, racing from whooping hordes of Indians to save the mail—wouldn't that be a grand way to live! Faster! Faster! With the way station just ahead! He'd leap from his horse, slap the saddlebags across a fresh mount, and jump into the saddle. Nothing would stop him! He reached to tug an arrow from his shoulder—

Mike sighed and shifted away from the long splinter in the side board that was digging into his back. Maybe he'd like working on a farm. He had promised Ma he was going to work hard and do his best.

A sudden wave of loneliness, so strong that it caused him to shiver, brought Ma's face to his mind, and he could see the terrible sorrow in her eyes. *I'll make you proud of me yet, Ma*, he vowed.

Mike glanced toward the front seat of the wagon and noticed Mr. Friedrich again scowling at his wife. He couldn't hear what was being said, but it sounded like the growl and snap of a mean, hungry dog. Mike hated to admit it to himself but Mr. Friedrich frightened him. Mrs. Friedrich wasn't so bad, so who knew? Maybe, if he minded his manners and did his work well, he might get along with both just fine. Maybe all the Friedrichs—even Gunter—would turn out to be better than he had first thought them.

Mike stared up at their rounded backs. The three of them were packed as closely together on the wagon seat as sausages in a crate. Before he knew it, his mind was racing with the words for a ditty: "Three fat sausages, Gunter in the middle; fry them on a griddle with a hey diddle diddle." Pleased with his rhyme, Mike grinned to himself. Some day he'd sing his song to his sister Frances. Wouldn't she get a good laugh from it!

Mike pictured his older sister at their parting. She'd cut her long, dark hair with his penknife after she'd heard that some families might take two boys. She had posed as a boy, desperately hoping to keep their youngest brother Petey with her, and her ruse had succeeded. Thinking they were adopting brothers, a family had chosen Frances and Petey together.

Would Mike ever see Frances again? Pushing away the thoughts that caused his throat to tighten with pain, he stretched out in the wagon and laid his head on his arms. Over and over he sang the new ditty to himself until he fell asleep.

"Hush! He will hear you, Hans!"
"He won't hear anything. He's sleeping."
"Why must you talk of Ulrich?"
The sharp fear in Mrs. Friedrich's voice jabbed Mike to wakefulness, but he kept his eyes closed, afraid to open them.

"This boy is a thief, as Ulrich was," Mr. Friedrich replied.

"Please, Hans, do not compare them. Give this boy a chance to prove—"

"A chance? Ulrich had every chance, yet what good did it do him?"

"Papa! When you talk of Ulrich, you get so angry it frightens me," Gunter whined.

Mrs. Friedrich began to whimper, too. "Remember, Hans, what your anger has lead to in the past," she said.

"Do not admonish me, Irma," Mr. Friedrich sputtered. "It is important that you understand my plans."

But Mrs. Friedrich hadn't finished. "No matter what he had done, Ulrich should not have died."

"Hush!" The word came out like an explosion.

The wagon seat creaked as someone turned to look at Mike. It was all he could do to lie quietly, pretending sleep, and swallow the cry of terror that rose in his throat. Who was Ulrich? And how had he died?

"He didn't hear, Papa. He is still asleep," Gunter reported.

Mike strained to listen again, but the Friedrichs lowered their voices. Because of their heavily accented speech, Mike could grasp only a word or two. What had Mrs. Friedrich meant when she said that no matter what he had done, Ulrich should not have died? Had someone killed him? Why? Mike was sure of only two things: Ulrich was a thief who had died because of what he had done, and Mr. Friedrich thought Mike was just like Ulrich. Mike's heart started pounding. He wanted to leap from the wagon and run, as fast as he could, back to St. Joseph and the safety of Andrew MacNair. But the Friedrichs would catch up with him, and then they would call him not only a thief but a runaway.

He tried to make himself relax and breathe evenly so it would be easier to think. Since he did not really know what had happened to Ulrich, and considering that his own situation was not good, it would be foolish to panic. The best plan would be to try to live with the Friedrichs, as Mr. MacNair and Mrs. Banks expected him to do, but to keep his eyes open and stay on the alert.

The wagon stopped so suddenly that Mike rolled against the end of the wagon bed, banging his knees and elbows. He sat up with a start to gape wide-eyed at a large house and an even larger barn. Who would have thought the Friedrichs were swells?

The two-story house gleamed with fresh white paint. Its windows sparkled in the late-afternoon light, and even the deep orange marigolds that lined the front of the house had been planted in tidy rows. The front door and the shutters were a bright blue, and at the windows Mike could see lace curtains. Beyond the house and barn stood the privy and some large and small outbuildings. Impressed, Mike whistled through his teeth.

Mrs. Friedrich awkwardly climbed from her perch, but Gunter remained on the wagon seat with his father.

"Out with you!" Mr. Friedrich called to Mike, who managed to grab his small packet of belongings and scramble from the wagon before it started up again with a jerk.

Two spotted mutts came running to sniff at Mike. "Wulf! And you, Bruna! Be gone with you!" Mr. Friedrich yelled. They quickly turned tail, dodged the hitching post, and ran around the corner of the barn.

"Come, Mike! Hurry!" Mrs. Friedrich said. "Hans will want his food ready and on the table as soon as he has taken care of the horses. I know how hungry he'll be."

Mike ran to catch up. "I'm hungry, too," he said. "We haven't eaten since breakfast."

"Ach!" she cried, "I should have thought. Well, no matter now. We'll have your stomach filled soon enough."

Just as they reached the door at the side of the

house, it was opened by a tall young woman with blond braids wound into a crown on top of her head. The sleeves of her cotton dress were rolled high on her tanned arms, and her stiff white apron nearly covered her faded skirt, which brushed the floor. She stood aside to let Mrs. Friedrich pass, but she looked Mike over carefully.

"You bring home a minnow, not a fish," she said and winked at Mike.

"Hush, Marta!" Mrs. Friedrich hissed and glanced quickly toward the barn. "Mr. Friedrich was upset enough because I had caused us to be late and the larger boys had been taken. If he hears you say that, it will only mean more trouble."

Mike's mouth opened in amazement as he glanced around the room. The kitchen was only a little smaller than the room that had been the Kelly family's entire home in New York City. The copper pots and cooking tools that hung on the wall gleamed in the light from the fire in the huge fireplace. And just a few steps from the fireplace was a large wood-burning stove! Two gigantic cupboards stood against the far wall next to a broad working table. A smaller table was placed near the side window, and on it was a blue bowl that held a clump of bright marigolds. A faint odor of lye soap clung to the bleached-wood floor. Mike had never seen anything to match this. How he wished he could show it to Ma and Megan and Frances. Wouldn't their eyes pop!

Mrs. Friedrich tugged off her coat and gloves and untied the ribbons on her hat that had become buried between her chins. "We must hurry and get supper on the table," she insisted.

"Since it's a cold supper, it's all but done," Marta said calmly. She looked at Mike but continued to speak to Mrs. Friedrich in the same rhythmic accent the rest of the family shared. "What is the name for this young carrottop?"

Mike took a step forward. He knew at once that he liked Marta and her friendly smile, in spite of the fact that she had called him a minnow and a carrottop.

"I'm Michael Patrick Kelly," he said, "but everybody calls me Mike." He turned to Mrs. Friedrich, who was smoothing down the folds of her voluminous dark skirt, and added, "I didn't know you had a daughter, ma'am."

Marta darted a sharp glance at Mrs. Friedrich and gave a wry smile. "Hardly a daughter," she muttered, but before Mrs. Friedrich could answer there was a loud stamping of feet on the outer stoop. In a moment a tall rangy man entered the room. The angles of his face were sharp against his ragged dark hair, and his eyes were deep-set under his brows. Mike guessed him to be nearly forty.

"Mrs. Friedrich," he acknowledged, then turned to Marta with a bow. "You heard me knock the soil from my boots, Marta, so now you won't be able to complain that I dirtied your clean floors." His gaze came to rest on Mike.

"Reuben, you haven't met young Michael Kelly," Marta said. "Mike, this is Reuben Starkey."

Reuben's eyebrows shot up. "This small twig is the boy you went to St. Joseph to fetch? The one who is to help work the farm?"

Mrs. Friedrich put a hand on Mike's shoulder and pursed her lips. "No matter that he's small. Michael is a poor, wretched orphan, and we have rescued him from a dreadful life."

Reuben's eyes lit with a mischievous twinkle. "*Poor naked wretches, wheresoe'er you are, that bide the pelting of this pitiless storm,*" he said.

Mike couldn't stand it any longer. Talking about him as though he weren't even there! And saying such rotten things! "You've got no right to call me a naked wretch!" he told Reuben. "I've got all my clothes on, same as you!"

"I didn't mean to offend you, Michael. I was merely

quoting from a play by William Shakespeare," Reuben said.

"Reuben's had schooling," Marta explained. "He's always reading poetry."

Reuben held out a hand. "I'm pleased to make your acquaintance, Michael."

Mike shook hands with Reuben. "I'm glad to meet you, too, Mr. Starkey." Mike turned to examine the room and nodded with satisfaction. "I see how it is now," he said. "I knew this house was too big for just one family. How many families live here?"

Marta put an arm around Mike's shoulders and pulled him closer to the fire in the big fireplace. "Reuben is the hired hand. He lives in a cabin out behind the barn. I have a room under the stairs, because I am working as the Friedrichs' serving girl."

"Oh, Marta"—Mrs. Friedrich's hands fluttered nervously—"you are like family."

"I am a serving girl," Marta said. "I came with the Friedrichs from Germany to this country and agreed to work to pay for my passage."

Marta's words were resentful, and Mike felt tension in the room. He tried to change the subject. "Will I live in a cabin, too, like Reuben?"

"Of course not," Mrs. Friedrich said. "You are to live with us as a son. You will have your own room upstairs. It's a very nice room, and I'm sure you'll find no fault with it."

Mrs. Friedrich didn't sound convincing, and—behind her employer's back—Marta rolled her eyes and shrugged her shoulders at Mike. He didn't understand why.

But Mrs. Friedrich's attention had shifted to Reuben. "Why aren't you in the barn helping Mr. Friedrich with the horses?" she asked.

"There's little more to do for the horses," Reuben

said, "so I thought I'd use the opportunity to meet my new helper."

Mrs. Friedrich sighed. "If only you had the same industry as Mr. Friedrich, how much more you could accomplish."

Reuben made a little bow and said, "There could only be one like Mr. Friedrich."

Mike saw the twinkle in his eyes, but apparently Mrs. Friedrich didn't. "Yah," she said. "You are right." She made a little shooing motion with her hands. "Well, go with you—back to the barn, where you can be of help."

As Reuben left, Marta said, "I'll show Mike his room now. It will give him a chance to take off his jacket and wash before he eats."

"Yes," Mrs. Friedrich murmured. "Of course." Glancing toward the back door, she urged, "But hurry, both of you! When Mr. Friedrich comes in, we must all be ready to sit at the table."

Mike's room was small, compared to what he had just seen, only large enough for a bed with a plain wooden bedstead, a slatted chair, and a low, red-painted chest. On the chest rested an oil lamp, a china pitcher filled with water, and a bowl. Curtains hung at the window, and Mike lifted them to see the barn, its big doors opened wide.

"Your room is not much," Marta said, "but I made sure that you had one of the best down quilts on your bed."

"The room looks grand to me," Mike assured her. He pushed down on the bedding, his hands almost disappearing into the thickly mounded quilt. "Oh!" he said. "I've never felt anything so soft!"

"Marta!" Mrs. Friedrich called sharply.

"Mrs. Friedrich is afraid of her husband," Mike blurted out.

"Oh, the man is all noise," Marta said. "He likes to

14

bluster like a cold north wind." She sniffed. "Mrs. Friedrich should have stood up to him from the very beginning. A wife should never cower in fear."

"Aren't you afraid of him?" Mike asked.

"No, I am not," Marta said, but Mike had heard her hesitate. "He has tried to shout at me, but I told him if he did it again I would leave. He knows I mean what I say, and I'm a hard worker and honest, so he doesn't want me to go."

"And you have to pay for your passage."

She smiled. "That's been taken care of. I'm staying on until someday I find a good man to marry. Then I'll have a home of my own." She ruffled Mike's hair and teased, "It's too bad you are not ten years older, with your own farmland and horses and cows. Unfortunately, a poor orphan could never be a good marriage prospect."

"I'm not an orphan," Mike said. "I have a mother. After Da died, Ma couldn't take care of us all, so she sent us west to find homes where we'd have better lives and enough food to eat. She wanted to help us, so she—she gave us away."

For just an instant Marta's blue eyes clouded with pity, and she reached out to touch Mike's shoulder. But Mrs. Friedrich called from below the stairs, "Marta! Where are you?"

Marta whispered to Mike. "There's no doubt you'll get plenty of good food here. Mr. Friedrich is known as a stingy man, but not when it comes to what goes into his stomach. Come. Forget the washing. We'd better hurry."

"Wait!" Mike said. "You've already been kind to me, so I hope you'll tell me something I've got to know." He lowered his voice to a whisper. "Please tell me, did Mr. Friedrich—did he ever kill someone?"

Marta gasped and took a step backward. "Why do you ask me that?"

"On our way here from St. Joseph I overheard them talking about someone called Ulrich who was dead."

Marta bent to clasp Mike's arms, holding him so tightly he wanted to cry out. "Whatever you do, never again mention Ulrich's name!"

"But Mr. Friedrich said I was just like Ulrich. Please tell me. Did he kill him? If he killed Ulrich he could—"

"That's enough!" Marta's face turned gray.

"Marta!" Mrs. Friedrich called, even more insistently.

Marta released Mike and, racing from the room, clattered down the stairs. Mike followed, trying to keep up with Marta's quick steps. At the foot of the stairs she grabbed his hand and pulled him down the hallway toward the dining room, where Mrs. Friedrich waited, her hands clasped at her waist. With one quick movement Marta smoothed down Mike's hair, ran through the room, and disappeared in the direction of the kitchen.

3

THE DINNER TABLE, which was covered with a fine white cloth, was laden with platters of sliced cold meats, heaping baskets of bread, and bowls that contained foods Mike had never seen. His stomach growled, his mouth began to salivate, and he leaned eagerly toward the table. He could hardly wait to eat. This was a feast he'd never even imagined could exist.

In less than a minute, Mr. Friedrich, with Gunter following, strode into the room. Mr. Friedrich contentedly patted his rounded stomach and murmured, "Fine, fine. The meal is ready."

He pulled out a chair at the head of the table and plopped into it, flicking out a large napkin and laying it across his lap. Mrs. Friedrich took the chair at the opposite end of the table, and Gunter lazily slid into a chair at the side. There was only one chair left. But there were three people for it—Marta, Reuben, and Mike—and Mike was puzzled. Where were they all supposed to sit?

"Who's the chair for?" Mike asked. "Reuben? Marta?"

"Reuben is only hired help," Mrs. Friedrich murmured, "and Marta prefers to eat in the kitchen."

Mr. Friedrich barked, "Sit down quickly, or leave the room!"

Mike dived into the remaining chair. He reached out a hand for his fork but stopped in embarrassment, tucking his hands out of sight on his lap, as Mr. Friedrich began to intone a long, involved blessing. In his prayer he somehow managed to ask for forgiveness for Mike, the sinner, who must atone for his evil ways. Humiliated, Mike felt his face burning. He knew Gunter was staring at him. If only he were big enough to take Gunter on! Behind the barn would be a good place. He'd roll Gunter's sneaky grin in the dirt, he would, until Gunter yelped for mercy.

Mr. Friedrich's loud "Amen" startled Mike and brought him back to the present. He was thankful that the prayer was finally over. The blessing Ma had always said was much more to Mike's liking. It was short and to the point and had no room in it for speaking ill of others.

Marta came to help serve, and Mr. Friedrich's plate was filled first. Then Gunter's. Then Mike's. Mrs. Friedrich was served last. That didn't seem right to Mike. Ma had always put the food on the table, then sat next to Da, and Da had reached for the choicest bits, putting them on Ma's plate and serving her first.

No one spoke as they ate. The three Friedrichs bent over their plates, rapidly shoveling food into their mouths. Occasionally Gunter belched, but neither of his parents seemed to notice. It certainly hadn't been like that at home!

Mike put the Friedrichs out of his mind. The food was more important. He tasted strange new dishes such as sliced potatoes mixed with a sweet-spicy sauce that smelled of onion and fried pork drippings. To his surprise, Mike loved it. When he put a bite of a golden spiced peach into his mouth, he closed his eyes and sighed with delight. He had never tasted anything so wonderful.

Mr. Friedrich helped himself and Gunter to seconds, emptying the bowls. He didn't offer more of anything to Mike, but Mike didn't mind. His stomach was so full that the waistband of his trousers dug into it.

"Good, good," Mrs. Friedrich murmured as she glanced at Mike's empty plate. "You have a good appetite, Michael. You'll soon begin to grow big and strong like Gunter."

Marta took the plates from the table, but no one moved. Mike wondered why but didn't dare to ask. Was Mr. Friedrich going to pray again?

But Marta brought in steaming cups of coffee and pitchers of milk, and she set a golden-crusted pie in front of Mr. Friedrich. He proceeded to cut large wedges, transferring them to small plates, which he passed to the others at the table. Mike couldn't imagine how he could possibly eat another bite of food, but the fragrance of lemon and sugar tickled his nose, and he took just one bite.

It was so wonderful and creamy, with its chewy topping, that Mike gobbled the entire piece, then leaned back in his chair, his belly stretched too tightly for him to bend forward. Ma had known what she was talking about when she'd said they'd have good food in the West. He'd write and tell her about all these delicious things he'd had to eat. He'd describe—

Mike stopped short, guiltily thinking of the boiled potatoes and cabbage that Ma would have for her noon meal. It didn't seem fair that Ma couldn't share all this. If he only had the choice, he'd rather have Ma and his brothers and sisters and potatoes and cabbage than everything else in the whole world. The shame of what he had done to separate his family smothered him like a fog. If he hadn't been arrested as a copper stealer, none of them would have been put on the Orphan Train. If Mr. Friedrich wanted to point out Mike as a sinner again, Mike would heartily agree with him.

But instead, Mr. Friedrich shoved back his chair and rose, giving a last swipe at his lips with his napkin before tossing it back on the table.

Mike quickly stood, too.

"You will help Marta clear the dishes from the table," Mr. Friedrich told Mike.

"Yes, sir," Mike said, glad to know what he was supposed to do next.

"Then you will help her to wash and dry them and put them away."

"Girl's work," Gunter snickered.

"It's work that needs to be done," Mr. Friedrich said. "Michael is properly grateful that we have taken him in to feed and clothe him and provide him with a fine home." His eyes narrowed as he stared down at Mike. "You *are* grateful, are you not?"

"Oh, yes, sir! I am!" Mike said.

"So you will work hard to repay us for our kindness."

Mike nodded. "I understand the agreement, Mr. Friedrich."

"Agreement?" Mr. Friedrich made a face of disgust. "We will hear no more of agreements." He leaned so close that Mike could see the red veins in his eyes and said, "I told you that I know how to handle boys. Remember?"

"Yes." Mike gulped.

"Very well. A boy who has been in trouble needs to be kept so busy he will not have time to get into further trouble. Good, hard work is a fine thing for any boy, but especially for you, Michael." Mr. Friedrich stepped back.

"Now—get to work with the dishes. Marta will welcome your help."

As Mr. and Mrs. Friedrich walked into the hallway, Mike turned to the table and picked up the nearest dish—the serving plate that held a large remaining wedge of the pie. Holding it carefully, he began to walk toward the kitchen, but he had gone only a few steps when his elbow was struck with such force that the plate flew out of his hands and smashed on the floor.

Gunter leapt away from him, shouting, "Papa! Come quickly! Mike threw the pie on the floor!"

Mr. and Mrs. Friedrich rushed back into the room. Marta appeared in the door to the kitchen, her eyes wide and startled.

Mike glared at Gunter, but he wasn't going to be a snitch. "It was an accident," Mike said. "Gunter saw what happened. I—I dropped the plate. I didn't mean to."

"It *wasn't* an accident!" Gunter said. "Mike thought that I had left the room, but I was watching. He threw the pie on the floor on purpose!"

"No, I didn't!" Mike cried. "Why would I?"

"He's a bad boy, Papa. Now he's calling me a liar," Gunter complained.

Mr. Friedrich shook his head sadly. "You have made a bad start here, Michael, and I had such hopes for you. I see that turning you from your former evil ways is going to be much harder than I had thought."

This was more than Mike could stand. "I'm *not* evil!" he shouted. "I didn't throw the pie plate on the floor. I'm sorry that I dropped it, and I'm sorry the plate is broken, but I didn't do what Gunter said I did."

Mr. Friedrich took a firm grip on Mike's arm. "We will go out to the barn, where I keep a leather strap," he said.

"Oh, Hans! No!" Mrs. Friedrich whimpered. "This is

21

only his first day!" Behind her back, where only Mike could see him, Gunter's smirk turned into a broad grin.

"A good beating will help Michael to learn how to behave," Mr. Friedrich said to his wife. "Trust me, Irma. I know now how to handle a boy like Michael."

Mike, his arm aching from Mr. Friedrich's tight grip, had to run to keep up with the man's long stride. He was sick with fear, and hot, angry tears ran down his cheeks. "Oh, Ma," he sobbed, "Ma!" even though he knew there was no way that his mother could hear or help him.

4

MIKE WOKE WITH a start the next morning to a loud thump on his door. "Out of bed! Quickly now! We will have no lazy boys lying about when there's work to be done!" Mr. Friedrich called.

Mike tried to jump out of bed, but he grabbed the bedstead for support, groaning as pain throbbed through the raised welts on his back and legs. The memory of the beating returned with a rush, and his eyes blurred with tears. He'd never been hit like that before. Occasionally he'd felt the sharp tap of a swell's walking stick or the flick of a cabbie's whip when he'd darted in someone's way, and he was used to the threats of bullies, but he'd always been able to outsmart them.

What was he going to do now?

He raised his head and brushed the tears from his face. "Mike, my lad," he said to himself, "you'll have to think sharp and fast, because it's sure that you'll not be accepting another beating like that ever again."

The moon had gone down, but it was still far too early for the sun to rise. Darkness pressed against the window. Mike, his eyes accustomed to the dimness, did not light the lamp. He poured water from the pitcher to the basin and splashed his eyes well. He didn't want them to know that he'd been crying. Wincing with each movement, he managed to dry his hands and face and pull on his clothes. He ran his comb through his hair, and in just a few minutes clattered down the stairs.

He ran toward the lights in the dining room, stopping abruptly just inside the door. Already the Friedrichs were eating.

Mrs. Friedrich patted at her mouth with her napkin and gave Mike a timid smile, but Mr. Friedrich, without raising his head, said, "After this, if you are late, you will eat in the kitchen with Marta and Reuben. For now, sit down quickly."

Mike hurried to his chair and put his napkin on his lap. Marta bustled into the room and placed in front of him a plate of sausages, ham slices, biscuits, hot fried apples, and two eggs, which stared at him like a pair of golden eyes.

"Thanks," Mike whispered to Marta and eagerly reached for his fork. The soreness in his body didn't keep him from being hungry.

But a large hand came down over his, and Mr. Friedrich glowered. "That one word was your prayer?"

"No, sir," Mike said. "I was thanking Marta."

"Then let us hear your prayer."

Mike bowed his head and said the blessing Ma and Da had taught him. As he came to the end, he looked up at Mr. Friedrich, hoping the man would now let him eat. The wonderful smells of the food were making his stomach rumble with hunger.

Finally the hand was pulled away. Mr. Friedrich said, "That will do," and went back to his food.

Mike bent over his plate and ate as greedily as the others. Occasionally he sneaked little side glances at them. None of the three seemed interested in him at all, not even Gunter. No one spoke of Mike's punishment the night before. Mike would have decided it was only a nightmare, except the ache in his back and legs proved the beating really had taken place.

Mr. Friedrich suddenly pushed his chair away from the table and stood. Before Mr. Friedrich could find fault with him, Mike dropped the last bite of biscuit on his plate and scrambled from his chair.

"Michael, today I am going to turn you over to Reuben Starkey," Mr. Friedrich said. "You will be in his charge." His eyebrows dipped into a scowl, and he tapped the back of his chair impatiently. "Unfortunately, Reuben can be a woolgatherer when he should be tending to business, but now that harvest is over, he's my only farmhand." He blinked, as though suddenly recalling that Mike was standing there, and continued. "Reuben knows he is to teach and train you in the jobs you will do on the farm to keep you busy and out of trouble. He will report to me on your progress, and if you have been lazy and shirked your chores, we will see that it does not happen again."

Mike's chin lifted, and he thought, *If it's beating me you're thinking of, then you've got another thing coming, because I'm not going to let that happen to me again!*

He realized that his face must have revealed his feelings, because Mr. Friedrich looked a little puzzled and said, less firmly, "Michael, our ways may seem different to you, but this is because you have not had a proper upbringing. No one has taught you that the devil makes use of idle hands, so it is up to us to teach you.

On a well-run farm there is much to do. You will work hard, but this will help to make a man of you." He paused. "I am a just man, Michael. I will not punish you unless you need punishment."

Mr. Friedrich stopped speaking and seemed to be waiting for something, so Michael, fighting a boiling resentment, muttered, "Yes, sir." Mr. Friedrich didn't know anything about his upbringing!

Mrs. Friedrich's hands fluttered as she squeaked, "Michael, you must say, 'Thank you, Mr. Friedrich.'"

Mike thought again of the barn and the strap. He had to live with these people. He'd have to follow their rules. He gripped his fists together behind his back, digging his nails into his hands. "Thank you, Mr. Friedrich," he echoed.

Mike glanced quickly at Gunter, but Gunter yawned widely and seemed completely uninterested in Mike. Maybe the beating Mike had suffered had been enough to satisfy Gunter. Mike hoped he'd have no more trouble from that tub of lard. In his mind he began to hum his sausage song and had to press his lips together to keep from laughing aloud.

"Get your coat and go to the barn," Mr. Friedrich said to Mike. "Reuben will be waiting for you."

As fast as he could, Mike raced up the stairs, snatched his jacket from the bedstead, and tore out to the barn. Light was beginning to streak the eastern sky, but the air was so cold it stung like a slap. He gasped and rubbed his arms, trying to get warm.

Wulf and Bruna ran toward him, their eyes wary, but Mike stopped and held out the backs of his hands for them to sniff. Satisfied, they accepted him and trotted at his side as he entered the barn.

The huge barn was almost as clean as the house, with the milk pails gleaming, the harness hanging over the rest of the tack in tidy rows, and the farm tools neatly stored at the far end of the barn. But here the smell of lye soap was overpowered by the fine, warm, sour smell of hay, which was piled high overhead in the loft and heaped on the floors of the stalls for the horses and cows.

Reuben was pouring a foaming bucket of milk into a large, gleaming milk can. As Mike came in, he looked up and swept a thick shock of black hair from his eyes. "Good morning," he said.

"Good morning, Mr. Starkey." Mike tried to keep his teeth from chattering.

"Is that the best they could give you for a warm coat?" Reuben asked.

"This is what I came in, sir," Mike said.

"You can forget the 'sir' and the 'Mr. Starkey,' " Reuben told him. He put down the bucket and strode over to join Mike. "Since we're going to work together, why don't you call me Reuben, and I'll call you Michael?" He reached out to shake his hand.

"Mike."

"Mike it is. Now, we'll see to finding a coat for you. It's time to take the cows to pasture, but they can wait." Reuben's long legs carried him swiftly out of the barn.

As Mike waited for Reuben to return, he looked around. There were half a dozen cows in the barn, big animals that looked at him with huge brown eyes as he came close. The nearest one shifted in her stall, her broad rump swinging in his direction. Mike quickly backed away.

Beyond the cows he could see two large-eared mules, and beyond them the horses that had pulled the wagon. The spotted gray was eating, but the tall black tossed his head up and down and stamped his feet, snorting and blowing loud blasts of air from his nose. Mike gazed at the horses with interest and wondered what it would be like to be perched high on the back of one of them, knees tight against the sweating flanks, hands entwined in the flowing mane, racing wildly over the hills, splashing through streams, the two of them free with no one to answer to.

"Fear no more the heat o' the sun, nor the furious winter's rages." Mike jumped as Reuben spoke behind him.

"Heat of the sun? It's not likely, with the sun still not high in the sky."

Reuben held out a warm woolen coat, cap, and knit gloves to Mike. "It's poetry, Mike. Shakespeare again. Have you never read the great poets?" As Mike gratefully struggled into the warm clothes, Reuben looked at him quizzically and added, "Can you read at all?"

"I can read. I even had a book of my own once," Mike said. "It was a dime novel—*Seth Jones, or Captive of the Frontier.* A grand story, full of adventure."

Reuben smiled. "Not exactly great literature, but at least you can read. Perhaps I can introduce some of the poets to you."

"Do they live around here, too?"

Reuben pulled a small, tattered book with a dark red cover from his coat pocket and tapped it. "They live in here," he said. "When we take a rest, I'll read to you from this book. A man is never alone if he's reading the words of great minds."

Mike fastened the last button on the coat and tugged on the gloves. "These are a good fit," he said.

"Mrs. Friedrich has laid by Gunter's outgrown clothes," Reuben said. "In this household nothing is ever wasted or given away freely. I'll ask Marta to put some of his clothes into the chest in your room." He reached into a bin and picked up a long switch, handing it to Mike. Then he whistled, and Wulf and Bruna scrambled over each other to reach his side.

"Use the switch on the cows' legs if they get out of line on the way to pasture." Reuben smiled. "You'll find

28

that the dogs do most of the work, but they're no good for opening or locking gates."

Mike jumped back as Reuben unfastened the gate on the first stall and the cow lumbered out. "I didn't know cows were so big!" He gasped and ducked as the cow's tail swished past his face.

"They won't hurt you unless you get close enough to get stepped on," Reuben said. He went from one stall to another, releasing the cows, who filed toward the open barn door as though they knew what was expected of them. Bruna trotted to one side, Wulf to the other, nudging and occasionally nipping to keep the big animals in line.

"Run ahead and open the gate," Reuben told Mike. Mike ran quickly, glad to get past the cows. He raced up a low hill to a fence made of posts laid in a zigzag pattern. Beyond the fence was a broad meadow, thick with grass and rimmed far off with deep green pines and smaller trees, their gold and orange leaves shimmering in the early morning light. Mike climbed on the gate to open the latch, then jumped down and shoved the gate wide.

As the cows went through, Reuben said, "Make sure that gate is tightly shut. These are prize cattle, which Mr. Friedrich is fond of reminding me of. He'd be mighty upset if they were to get loose and wander down the road."

"Will we go with the cows?" Mike asked.

"The cows will take care of themselves," Reuben answered. "No, you have other tasks to learn. There's water to bring into the house from the well and wood to chop and pile. There'll be plenty of field work, from planting to harvesting, and you'll help care for all the farm animals—the horses, cows, hogs, and pigs, even Mrs. Friedrich's chickens."

"Pigs?" Mike asked. "Where are the pigs and chickens?"

As though to answer him, a rooster crowed near the

barn. Mike turned to look down the hill at the house, barn, vegetable garden, and buildings that were set on the land. "What are all those small houses?" he asked.

Reuben chuckled. "The smallest one, which I'm sure you found right away, is the privy." As Mike nodded, Reuben continued. "To your left is the smokehouse— see, over there. That's where the meat is cured and hung. Nearby is the butcher shed." He continued to point. "At the far side of the barn is the chicken house. See it?"

"Yes," Mike said. "And way over there are the hogs."

"That building just behind the house is an outdoor kitchen to use during the summer's heat. Near it is the well, and the door at a slant to the ground leads to a root cellar where beans, corn, squash, potatoes, and all the vegetables and fruit that are raised here are stored. Over there's the cabin where I live, with room in it for another hand, although Mr. Friedrich is tightfisted when it comes to pay, and my only other help left the end of last week."

"Is that why I'm here?" Mike asked.

Reuben pursed his lips and rubbed his chin. "Just between you and me," he said, "I do believe that Mr. Friedrich was more interested in finding unpaid help than aiding a poor orphan boy." He shook his head. "Unfortunately, you're not big or strong enough for some of the jobs."

"But I'm willing to work hard," Mike said quickly.

"I believe you are." Reuben studied Mike's face and added, "I'll teach you, Mike, and help where I can. Your life with the Friedrichs may not be what you had hoped for. Mr. Friedrich demands hard work from everyone, but he pushes himself to work even harder. However, the Friedrichs will give you a warm bed and good food, which is more than many orphans would have."

"I'm not an orphan," Mike said. "I have a ma. She'll always be my ma, and someday I'm going to see her again. I know I will!"

"Determination and hope are good for the soul," Reuben said.

"Did one of your poets say that?" Mike asked.

"No, I did," Reuben said. He put a hand on Mike's shoulder, but Mike winced.

In answer to Reuben's puzzled look, Mike said, "I'm a bit sore in the back, that's all."

"Well, our next chore might loosen those sore muscles. We've got a barn to shovel out and wash down."

"I'm game for it," Mike said.

Reuben smiled and led the way down the hill. "While we're working, we'll talk," he said. "I'd like to hear about your journey west."

Mike breathed quickly as he trotted to keep up with Reuben. He liked Reuben, and he wanted to be his friend. But sooner or later Reuben would hear that he had been a copper stealer. Mike realized he'd rather Reuben heard it from him. "There's a lot to tell," he said.

"There's a lot I already know," Reuben said.

Mike looked up as they entered the barn. "You mean about—about why my ma sent my brothers and sisters and me to the West?"

"Every man has a past," Reuben said. "What counts is his future." He handed Mike a stiff broom made from tightly knotted and tied reeds. "I'll shovel. You sweep. And you can tell me more about that outlaw on the train. I never heard of anyone stealing from an outlaw."

"He had taken Mrs. Banks's ring," Mike said.

"Katherine Banks? Oh, yes. That pretty lady who runs the general store in St. Joseph." Reuben bent to scoop large mounds of hay and dung into a handbarrow. "Tell me all about it."

"It was sometime after we left a place called Hannibal," Mike said. "Everything happened all at once. The train stopped so fast the wheels made an awful screeching noise, and some people started yelling and scream-

31

ing. There were a lot of men on horseback. One of them poked his long gun into the window of our car, and a bearded man with a gun ran in through the door. He held out a bag and told us to drop our money and jewelry into it. Mrs. Banks asked the outlaw if he'd let her keep the ring her husband had given to her because it meant a lot to her, but he wouldn't."

Mike paused, and Reuben said, "Go on."

"Mrs. Banks looked crushed—about ready to cry—so I—I rushed into the outlaw," Mike explained, ducking his head as he added, "the way I'd learned to do it in New York." Reuben didn't respond. Mike stepped around him into the first stall and attacked the scattered dust and dirt with his broom. Finally he continued. "When the outlaw staggered back to catch his balance, I reached into the bag where the passengers had dropped their money. I got the feel of Mrs. Banks's ring, so I grabbed it, along with a fistful of bills. Mrs. Banks was glad to get her ring back, and Captain Taylor—who's a mighty fine man—said he was proud of me, but some of the passengers—there was one, a Mr. Crandon—were angry. They said I shouldn't have come on the Orphan Train, since I was a pickpocket who couldn't be trusted. They wanted to send me back to New York."

"And you wouldn't want to go back to New York City?"

Reuben's wide sweeps with the shovel had taken him far ahead of Mike, so Mike rushed to catch up. "No," Mike said. "The judge told me if I was sent back, I'd go to Tombs Prison."

Reuben stopped and stared at Mike. Finally he said, "Then you must never go back."

"I stole because we were hungry," Mike said. "But I promised Ma and I promised myself I would never steal again."

Reuben took Mike's broom and swept the pile of hay

and dust and crumbs onto his shovel and from there into the handbarrow.

"I wish no one had to know about it," Mike said.

Reuben smiled wryly. *"When in disgrace with fortune and men's eyes, I all alone beweep my outcast state—"* He stopped and shook his head. "No, Mike. Wrong poet. You're not alone."

"I feel alone."

"You've got a friend—right here." With a long finger, Reuben poked his own chest.

Tears came to Mike's eyes, and his throat was so tight it hurt to speak. "Thanks," Mike said. He rubbed hard at his eyes with the backs of his hands.

Reuben's voice was cheerful. "And you've got a new family who'll come in time to appreciate you, I'm sure. Soon you'll be going to school and playing games with Gunter."

Mike shivered with anger as he thought of what Gunter had done to him. "Gunter hates me and has already caused trouble for me. He's a stinking barrel of tallow!" Mike muttered. "He's a hog. No, he's worse than a fat hog."

"Here, here now," Reuben said. "Nothing good comes from that kind of talk. Get yourself up into the loft. You'll find a rake up there. You can use it to toss fresh hay down into the stalls."

Mike scrambled up the ladder, eager to see the loft. But as he reached the top and peered over the rim, he found himself looking directly into Gunter Friedrich's narrowed, angry eyes.

5

MIKE OPENED HIS mouth to speak, but he could only gasp.

"Stinking barrel of tallow, am I? Fat hog?" As Gunter struggled to his feet and stumbled toward the ladder, Mike scrambled and slid to the ground as fast as he could.

Gunter was right behind him. Fists out, he advanced on Mike, but Reuben stepped between them, a strong hand on Gunter's arm. "We'll have no fighting," he said firmly.

"I heard what he called me," Gunter snapped.

"You were spying! That's why!" Mike answered back.

"Was not! Pa sent me up there to spread the hay." He shook off Reuben's arm and glared at Mike, eyes narrowing as he spat out, "So! If you get sent back to New York, you'll go to prison! That's good to know."

Mike fought against the cold chill that shivered down his backbone. "I'm not going back," he said.

"We'll see about that," Gunter said. He turned and stomped out of the barn.

Mike looked up at Reuben and stammered, "D-do you think he'll tell his father what I said?"

Reuben shrugged. "If he does, it's not enough to make Friedrich send you back."

Mike closed his eyes, whispering to himself, "But he might beat me again."

"He's beaten you? Mr. Friedrich?" Reuben's voice was so sharp that Mike was startled. "Is that why your back was sore?"

Mike nodded. "I'm afraid of Mr. Friedrich," he admitted.

"The man has a fierce, quick temper," Reuben said. "More than a few times he's tried to take it out on me."

Mike glanced toward the open barn door and lowered his voice. "Do you know if he—if he ever killed a man? Someone named Ulrich?"

Reuben scowled as he thought. "I haven't heard the family talk of anyone named Ulrich, and as for gossip, I pay it no heed. In this country a man can leave his past behind and never look back."

Mike quickly said, "Don't think I sneaked and spied, like Gunter. The three of them talked loudly enough to wake me when we were coming here from St. Joe. They thought I was asleep in the wagon. They talked about Ulrich. He was a thief, but now he's dead. I only heard part of what they were saying, but I know that much. And I suspect that Mr. Friedrich killed him."

"You only heard part of a conversation, yet you're ready to put together a whole story? It might be as bold and daring as the stories you've read in the dime novels."

Mike saw the corners of Reuben's mouth twitch, and he had to smile himself. "I guess I was letting fear get the best of me," he said, "and I admit I'm always one for a good tale." But, in spite of his brave tone, he shivered. "I am afraid of the man," he murmured. "I don't want him to beat me again."

Reuben squatted, bony knees akimbo, his deep-set

35

eyes drilling into Mike's. "I'll do what I can to help you, but I have no influence with Mr. Friedrich. He doesn't much like me and puts up with my 'unproductive book reading and woolgathering'—as he calls it—because I'm the only one he can find who will work for his meager wages."

"Why do you work for low wages?" Mike asked. "Aren't there any other jobs?"

Reuben stood, tugging down his coat, and smiled. "I don't need much besides food and keep, and my work here is only temporary. There's a fine job waiting for me back at the river, when I'm ready for it."

"At the river?" Mike was puzzled.

"I worked on flatboats for many years," Reuben said, "until I came down with the pleurisy and the doctor told me to find a job away from the dampness of river mists. But I miss the river, and I'll be going back someday."

"Not soon?" Mike could feel his chin trembling. He didn't want to lose the only friend he had in this place.

"Not soon," Reuben answered. He glanced at the loft. "Back to work. Quickly, now! We have much to get done before noon."

By the time the noon bell clanged loudly, Mike was dirty and sweaty and glad to stop to wash his hands and face in the basin of water set outside the back door. In spite of his big breakfast, he was ravenous.

Again Mr. Friedrich said a long prayer, but Mike didn't pay much attention. He kept sneaking looks at Gunter. Once he caught Gunter peering at him, a smile flicking at his lips. Mike quickly closed his eyes and bowed his head over his clasped hands.

Mike's thoughts were in a turmoil. *Did Gunter tell his father what I said? Mr. Friedrich doesn't seem to be angry with me. Maybe Gunter hasn't told him. But Gunter wants to get me into trouble. So why hasn't he told his father?*

Mike opened just one eye for a quick peek at Gunter, who sat piously with downcast eyes. He was sure that Gunter had something in mind. Mike knew he'd have to be very careful.

At last loud "Amens" were said. Mike joined in quickly. Mr. Friedrich began heaping food onto the plates, and finally Marta placed Mike's serving in front of him. He moaned with pleasure as he breathed in the mingled fragrances of beef—boiled with spices and doughy dumplings—buttered carrots, beans cooked with lumps of fat pork, cabbage salad with a creamy dressing, and thick slices of dark wheat bread, hot from the oven. "Oh!" Mike said. "Marta's a wonderful cook!"

Marta giggled, and Mrs. Friedrich said, "Marta does the washing and peeling and chopping chores. *I* am the only cook in this house."

Mike swallowed a bite of beef, unbelievably juicy and tender, and sighed. "Mrs. Friedrich, you are the best cook in the whole world." He spread butter on his bread and watched it melt and soak into the warm slice before he tore off a piece and popped it into his mouth.

Mrs. Friedrich's cheeks dimpled, her skin pink, her eyes twinkling with delight. "Thank you, Michael. Maybe some of the food you like so much will help you to fill out. Already I see more color in your face. You will soon be a fine, handsome boy." She looked to her husband for agreement, but his head was down, his right hand gripping his fork as he shoveled food into his mouth.

Mrs. Friedrich turned back to Mike. "What are your favorite things to eat? You must tell me."

"Whatever it is you've cooked," Mike said.

She giggled. "Don't tease me, Michael."

"I'm not teasing," he said. "Sure and if the rest of the world knew about the fine foods you set on your table, there'd be people with plates in their hands lined up outside your door just begging for a taste."

She laughed happily. "Oh, Michael, you are so funny! But you did not give me an answer to my question."

Mike paused to think a moment. "Well, I always like a bit of sweet, and sausages are fine."

"What did your mother cook?"

"Potatoes and cabbage and sometimes squash or carrots. Boiled meat when—when we could come by it." He stopped, embarrassed by the surprise in her eyes. Mike could feel Gunter staring at him, and he refused to look in Gunter's direction.

"Are you going to talk or eat?" Mr. Friedrich asked.

Mike knew that was an order, not a question. He bent to his plate and ate as fast as he could, trying to keep up with Mr. Friedrich.

Before long Marta took the plates from the table and brought in a bowl of apples cooked with syrup and covered with a thick, flaky, golden-brown piecrust. In her other hand she carried a pitcher of yellow cream. While she ladled spoonfuls of the apples into bowls, pouring cream over them, Mike heard the sound of hoofbeats.

Mr. Friedrich sat erect, listening too, but Marta went to the window, pulled back the lace curtains, and looked out.

"Oh!" she said, her cheeks turning red. "It's three of the Blair brothers."

"The Blairs!" Mr. Friedrich threw down his napkin and scowled. "They're all young hotheads! It's the likes of those settlers, come up from the South, that will send this country into war." He gave a longing glance toward his dish of apples and pushed back his chair. "Well— send them into the parlor, and we'll see what it is they want."

Marta didn't move. As she fumbled with her apron, she mumbled, "It could be they have come to see me and not you, Mr. Friedrich. I'll find out."

38

In a few moments, the door between the dining room and the kitchen was thrown open, and a tall, lean, deeply tanned young man with sun-bleached hair stepped through. His trousers were tucked into sturdy black boots, and his dark jacket looked as though it had been made of homespun wool. He held a battered felt hat in his hands and nodded pleasantly. "Mr. Friedrich," he said, then nodded to Mrs. Friedrich. "Ma'am." His smile included Gunter and Mike.

"What is it, Corey Blair?"

Mr. Friedrich's voice sounded irritated. Corey Blair quickly apologized. "Sorry to interrupt your meal," he said. "Me and my brothers are ridin' over to Kansas."

"Hasn't there been enough bloodshed along the border?" Friedrich snapped. "You want to add more?"

"Those easterners who live in the territory are workin' to make Kansas a free state," Corey said. "We got to keep 'em from doin' it."

"What does it matter?" Mr. Friedrich's face grew so red and puffed out, it looked to Mike as though it might explode. "We are leading a comfortable life. Why should the situation change?"

Corey looked surprised. "It's bound to change," he said. "Those Kansas jayhawkers want to take away our right to own slaves."

Mike's mouth opened in amazement. He had never met anyone who believed in slavery. He couldn't understand why anyone would.

Mr. Friedrich lumbered to his feet. "You don't even own slaves! Why do you get involved in this trouble?"

"Because Missouri is a slave state, and my brothers and me—we're loyal to Missouri. What we do on our own land is our own business!"

Mike shuddered. Missouri was a slave state? No one had told him that. He was thankful that Mr. Friedrich didn't own any slaves.

39

"Foolish, foolish!" Mr. Friedrich thundered. "Don't you know what is happening to Missouri and Kansas? Those ignorant raiders on both sides, with their causes and their so-called loyalties, are stealing from honest people. They're burning houses and murdering. Is that what you want to do?"

Corey shifted from one foot to the other. "I don't think you understand, Mr. Friedrich."

"Don't understand? Oh, yes! I understand. I understand that someday some young men like you—with hot blood in their brains instead of good sense—will ride through my land, burning my barn and stealing my money before they even stop to think about what they are doing!"

Mrs. Friedrich gasped and put a hand to her throat.

"Naw. It's not going to be like that," Corey answered, and Mike let out a breath of relief.

"If we have war, it will be you and those who think like you who will cause it!"

"Not me!" Corey's eyebrows shot up in amazement. "It's Abraham Lincoln who's goin' to start a war, if he gets elected."

"But you are helping it to happen. If this country is split by war, what will you and those like you do then?"

Corey immediately began to perk up. His eyes sparkled. "Me? Why, I'll go and fight, by G—" He broke off and looked at Mrs. Friedrich. "I'll fight," he said.

Mr. Friedrich sighed. "So, why are you here now? What is it you want from me?"

Corey twisted the brim of his hat and shrugged. "Well, nothin' really, Mr. Friedrich. We—uh—that is, I come to say good-bye to Marta."

"To Marta?" Mr. Friedrich's words were an echo of Mike's own thoughts. "Why should you want to say good-bye to Marta?"

"Well—uh—I seen Marta at our church supper couple'a months ago and spoke with her. And since then, on

40

Sundays, when she only has to work half a day and you and your missus are at your church, I been ridin' over to sit in your kitchen with her and talk and sometimes go walkin'."

Mr. Friedrich looked even more uncomfortable than Corey. "This nonsense must stop" he said. "Marta is not ready to be courted."

"She's of marriage age," Corey said. "And bein' the oldest, I'll someday be gettin' a parcel of my pa's farm to work on my own."

Mike wasn't much interested in marriage talk, so he quietly gobbled the last couple of bites of his stewed apples and, with his spoon, carefully scraped every bit of the syrup from the bowl.

Mr. Friedrich whirled toward his wife. "What do you know of all this?" he demanded.

"N-No more than you," she stammered.

"Mr. Blair!" Friedrich advanced on Corey, who stubbornly held his ground. "Go on your way—you and your brothers who are so intent on making trouble!"

Corey looked surprised. "I don't aim to make trouble here."

"You have always been a troublemaker."

"Oh," Corey said, "so that's it. You're still mad about the time we accidentally set your privy afire."

Mr. Friedrich's face darkened even more. "It was not that many years ago. You were and are still an irresponsible boy!"

"That ain't fair nor right," Corey began, but Mr. Friedrich waved his hand in dismissal.

"Remember this—you are no longer welcome on my property!"

Without a word, Corey turned and stalked back into the kitchen. For a few moments his angry voice could be heard. After a short silence, the back door slammed.

41

Mike could hear horses' hooves kicking up the gravel in the road.

"Surely Marta would not be so foolish as to marry that idiotic young man!" Mr. Friedrich grumbled.

Mrs. Friedrich was almost as pale as the napkin she was twisting. "Why would she want to leave us? We provided her passage. We made a home for her. Where are her loyalties?"

"You must talk to her," Mr. Friedrich said.

"Hans?" Mrs. Friedrich's fingers fluttered once more to her neck. "What you said about men coming here to burn and steal—your gold watch, my mother's silver brooch. What if? . . ."

"It was Corey Blair who set fire to the privy?" Gunter grinned.

"Hush," Mrs. Friedrich said. "It's not a thing to laugh about. He and his brothers were on our land smoking with some of the farmhands. It made your father furious." She leaned toward her husband. "Hans, will all that you said really happen?"

"I would not have said it if I did not believe it *could* be."

Mike noticed that the skin on Mrs. Friedrich's knuckles was stretched tightly as she gripped the edge of the table. He felt sorry for her. "You could put your money in the bank," Mike suggested. "The swells in New York do."

"Never!" Mr. Friedrich exploded. "That would be a sure way to lose it! I do not trust paper money, and I do not trust banks. And don't interfere, Michael."

"Hans," Mrs. Friedrich whispered, "what should we do? Marta knows about . . . If she should tell Corey Blair. . ."

Mr. Friedrich's gaze shifted in Mike's direction, and he scowled. "Irma! Be silent! You should not talk of such things in front of others!"

"I'm sorry," Mrs. Friedrich whispered. "I'm so afraid,

I did not think. Corey Blair is now angry with you. What if he should come back?"

"Corey is nothing but a fool. He won't harm us." Mr. Friedrich's brow creased even more deeply. "Will you stop quivering and whimpering like a small child, Irma? There is no need for you to be afraid. I have taken care of this family with prudence and wisdom, and I will continue to do so."

His glance fell on Mike. "Why are you still sitting here when there is much work to be done?"

Mike gulped, unable to answer. No matter what he did or didn't do, he ended up in trouble.

"Before you go back to work, Michael," Mr. Friedrich grunted, "help Marta clear the plates from the table. I trust you have learned to do the job properly."

"Yes, sir," Mike said. From the corner of his eye he saw Gunter's smirk. Was Gunter really stupid enough to try the same trick twice? Mike wouldn't be fooled again.

Mike puttered at the table, scraping and stacking the bowls, while Mr. and Mrs. Friedrich left the room. Gunter slowly moved to stand near Mike. Mike grinned at Gunter, then ran empty-handed to the kitchen. "Marta," he said, "I'm going to help you clear the dishes."

"Thank you," Marta muttered. Her eyes sparked with anger as she stomped in front of Mike into the dining room.

Gunter stepped out of the way, surprised, but Marta shoved a stack of bowls into his hands. "Here," she said. "You may as well help, too. Take these to the kitchen."

"Papa didn't say I had to" Gunter complained.

Marta's nose almost touched his, and her words were firm. "*I* said you had to. Would you like to make more of this?"

Grumbling, Gunter headed toward the kitchen.

In just a few minutes the table was cleared. As Marta slammed the utensils into a pan of hot, soapy water, she said, "Out, out the both of you! I thank you for your help, but now you can help me by leaving me to my work. Mike, Reuben wants you to help him cut wood. You'll find him up the hill."

Outside the kitchen Gunter glared at Mike. Mike could almost hear Frances warning, "Use your common sense, Mike! Hold your tongue!" but he couldn't keep still. He made a face at Gunter and said, "You were stupid to try the same trick again. I was ready for you."

"You won't be ready the next time!" Gunter sputtered. He took a threatening step close to Mike, his pudgy hands clenched into fists. "I'll think up something else—something you'll never expect."

Marta opened the door and shouted at them, "Why are you just standing there? Do you want more trouble? Go along! Now!"

Mike turned and ran up the hill to join Reuben. He knew he had just made a big mistake.

6

MIKE HEARD REUBEN before he saw him. He followed the rhythmic thud of ax against wood through the grove of trees that topped the hill. At the edge of a small clearing dappled with sunlight and shade, Mike stopped. Reuben, his coat off, his shirt dark with sweat, swung the ax high in an arc to come thudding down on a fallen tree. In just one motion, as the wood groaned and cracked, he tugged the ax from the cleft it had made, circled it back and up, and slammed it down again.

Mike hesitated to break the rhythm, but as he stepped forward, a twig snapped underneath his shoe, and Reuben looked up. Slowly he lowered the ax and smiled.

"How long does it take to finish a plate of apples and cream?"

"It wasn't the food that kept me," Mike said. "It was the riders who came to see Marta."

"Riders?" Reuben wiped away the sweat that was dripping from his shaggy eyebrows into his eyes.

Mike told Reuben how the meal had been interrupted. He couldn't help shaking his head a little when he got to the part about how Mrs. Friedrich had been so afraid that thieves would come for her jewelry and the Friedrichs' money.

"Who steals my purse steals trash," Reuben said.

"Oh, no! Not trash," Mike said. "Since Mrs. Friedrich was so worried, they must have a great deal of money."

"The Friedrichs are no different from the other hardworking farmers who came from German states to settle in Missouri. They mistrust paper notes and insist on dealing in gold and silver coinage. Furthermore, they have a deep suspicion of banks, so they keep what they call their 'hard money' at home."

Reuben rubbed the back of his neck and took a firm grip on his ax. "I'm going to break up this dead hickory, and you can gather the twigs and limbs and chunks of kindling and bind them into bundles." He pointed. "You'll find twine over there, under that pine tree."

Mike worked hard, occasionally pausing to arch his back, which was feeling much less sore, and stretch and knead his neck and shoulders. Reuben did the same.

Reuben finally called, "Let's take a rest." Laying down the ax, he flopped onto his back. He rested his head on his crossed arms, and stared up at the sky. "There's a difference in the sky over land and the sky over water."

Mike sat on the ground, pulled out his pocketknife, and whittled chips from a nearby twig. "Did your poet Shakespeare say that?"

"No. It's something that every river boatman knows."

"Tell me about that kind of boat you worked on," Mike said.

"The flatboat? It's a long boat with a small cabin, two sweeps on each side and—"

"What are sweeps?"

"Oars. Poles with flat ends. Each boat carries a crew

to man the sweeps, a captain, and a cook. Flatboats are built and caulked at the riverbank, loaded with cargo, and floated down to towns much farther south where there's a good market for the potatoes or corn or whatever the boat carries. The boat's sold there, along with the cargo, and the crew catches the next stern or side-wheeler and sails back up the river again to start over."

"That doesn't sound very exciting," Mike said. "Not as exciting as riding for the pony express."

Reuben chuckled. "But it is. There are hidden sand-bars, and fast currents, and in some places enough boats of all kinds to run down any craft not quick enough to squeak through. Then there are raftsmen, who'll pick a fight with anyone and who are the worst kind of river rats. There are river pirates to worry about, too. They'd as soon steal your cargo and leave you for dead as not. And if you manage to get to where you were headed, you've got to contend with the merchants who try to drive such a hard bargain for your goods as to make the whole trip not worth the while."

In his mind's eye Mike could see a swift boat bearing down on his flatboat. It was filled with pirates, scarves wrapped around their heads and knives gripped between their teeth. With wild shouts they brandished swords and leapt to the deck of the flatboat. But Mike was too quick for them. Raising his sweep from the water, he laid about with it, knocking pirates right and left into the water while his mates on the flatboat cheered.

Mike heard a crack of a twig in the woods nearby and looked up sharply, but he didn't see anything. Probably a squirrel or a rabbit, he decided, and turned back to Reuben. "Wouldn't it be safer to work on one of the big steamboats?"

"Steamboat hands have their problems, too," Reuben replied. "Each man to his own choice, and mine is the

47

flatboat." He sighed. *"Nur einen Sommer gönnt, ihr Gewaltigen!"*

Mike stared at him. "What does that mean?"

"Only one summer grant me, you mighty ones! It's German. Hölderlin—my mother's favorite poet. My mother was German. Hölderlin loved his country so much."

"Are you German like the Friedrichs?" Mike asked.

"Not like them. But my heritage stems from their country."

Mike heard a small noise again, but it was farther away. He listened again. Maybe a deer, from the sound of it. Too heavy for a smaller animal. The gentle noises of the country were so different from the ones he knew so well in the city, but one by one Mike was beginning to recognize them.

Reuben's long legs bent like a pretzel as he scrambled to his feet. "Up, up," he said, "and back to work. You keep tying while I get one of the mules to help us cart these bundles to the shed."

The rest of the day Mike worked hard to keep up with Reuben. There were the animals to care for and feed, tools to mend, the vegetable garden to hoe, and wood to carry to the outdoor bin and those beside the fireplaces. When Marta finally rang the bell to call the men to supper, Mike was so exhausted he wanted only to fall into bed.

"Don't anger Mr. Friedrich," Marta whispered to Mike. "Wash up—all the way to the elbows—comb your hair, and come to the table." She winked and gave him a friendly pat on the back. "Be quick about it, too!"

Mike splashed his face and arms with water, shivering as he scrubbed hard with the lump of lye soap. In a way, he hated to remove all the warm, comfortable smells of the cows and barn and fresh-chopped wood and meadow grasses. This country life wasn't half bad, if you didn't mind a more-than-generous share of hard work.

Mike wondered how his brother Danny was faring. Did he have cows to send to pasture and bring back to the barn at night? Wouldn't it have been grand if they could have worked side by side? But instead they'd been parted, and he didn't know when he'd ever see his brother again.

Mike thought about the couple who had chosen Danny and Peg. They looked pleasant and he hoped they were good people, but he didn't know enough about them to tell for sure. Would they make a good home for Danny and Peg? Would they know how badly Danny had missed Da, and how much he needed the love of a father? If Danny ever needed his big brother, would he be able to let Mike know? Mike rubbed hard at his face with the linen towel. He knew enough to hurry without a warning from Marta and pushed thoughts of his family to the back of his mind.

Throwing a longing glance toward his comfortable bed, Mike ran from his room and down the stairs, arriving in the dining room before the others. He overheard voices in the parlor.

"But they were, Papa." It was Gunter, insisting. "I couldn't hear all they said, but I certainly recognized German words. Reuben was speaking to Mike in German!"

Mike was startled. It hadn't been a deer. The noise he had heard in the woods had been Gunter, spying!

"Michael! You are here already!" Mrs. Friedrich spoke loudly, and there was sudden silence in the next room. Mr. Friedrich, Gunter close behind him, appeared in the doorway. They stared at Mike with such deep suspicion that Mike frantically tried to think of the right thing to say.

"I got here first, which probably means I'm the hungriest!" He tried to sound cheerful and hoped his laughter didn't sound as false to them as it did to himself.

49

"Why did you not come into the parlor to join us?" Mr. Friedrich demanded.

"In the parlor? Oh, is that where you were?" Mike asked. He saw the muscles in Mr. Friedrich's jaw begin to relax.

"Be seated," Mr. Friedrich barked, apparently satisfied that Mike hadn't overheard Gunter. Mike gladly slipped into his chair.

Mike folded his hands for Mr. Friedrich's prayer. He tried to concentrate, and at first he did, but as Mr. Friedrich droned on and on, Mike's thoughts focused on the mealtimes his true family had shared in New York City. He could picture everyone seated around the table.

Ma would bow her head to say the blessing, sometimes reaching out to tap a hand that was trying to snatch a crumb. Mike couldn't figure out how Ma could see with her eyes closed, but she never missed a trick. Their meals together—even though since Da had died the portions were often too small to fill their stomachs— were usually noisy, cheerful times, with each of the Kellys having something to say and not always waiting for a turn in which to say it.

Mike saw Ma's ready smile as she helped Petey, the youngest Kelly. He thought of Peg, who never could seem to sit still, even while she was eating, and Danny, with his mischievous grin, and Megan, with her gentle ways, and Frances Mary, who tried to be as grown-up as Ma, but who could easily collapse into a fit of giggles anytime Mike had a mind to make silly faces.

Suddenly Da's sunburned face, with the laugh crinkles around his eyes, came into Mike's mind so strongly that he clenched his hands together tightly. *Oh, Da*, he thought, *the troubles began when you left us! Why did you have to die?*

The memory hurt so much that Mike's stomach ached, and tears rushed to his eyes, some of them escaping before he could rub them away.

50

"Michael." Mr. Friedrich was calling his name.

Mike immediately came back to the present, terrified that Mr. Friedrich would be angry again. But the man was actually smiling.

"I see that your heart was touched." Mr. Friedrich nodded with self-satisfaction. "I believe there is hope for you if you will keep in mind the fearful picture I have just described of the afterlife that waits for those who will not mend their wicked ways."

Mike nodded. He pulled a cotton handkerchief from his pocket and blew his nose, hoping he could cover the surprise that must have shown on his face. That was a narrow squeak!

Marta carried in a huge tureen filled with a thick soup, and dark wheat bread and butter to go with it.

Mrs. Friedrich's eyes twinkled as she watched Mike eat. "Do you like my soup, Michael?" she whispered.

Mike closed his eyes, savoring the deep, rich taste of the mingled vegetables, spices, and beef. "It's far too good to be called soup," he murmured.

She giggled. "There's warm gingerbread to follow, and, just for you, the rest of last night's spiced peaches."

Gunter raised his head from his soup plate. "I want peaches, too."

"There is only enough for one portion," Mrs. Friedrich said, "and Michael shall have it. He must fatten up and grow strong and tall."

Gunter glared at Mike, but Mike didn't care. He was too sleepy now to worry about Gunter, and those peaches had been awfully good. He did notice that during the rest of the meal Gunter wore a scowl. Gunter's expression grew darker when Mr. Friedrich finally laid his fork on his empty plate and said, "Get to bed now, Gunter. With school tomorrow, you must get an early start."

"School?" Mike's eyes flew open, and he sat up eagerly. At last! Andrew MacNair had told them they'd have schooling, and Mike couldn't wait until it started.

"We have a schoolhouse, just two miles away," Mrs. Friedrich began to explain. "The teacher is a fine young woman who boards with—"

"Enough!" Mr. Friedrich interrupted. "Michael will not be going to school."

Mike forgot to be cautious and blurted out, "But we were told that we were to get schooling until we were fourteen."

Mr. Friedrich shrugged. "You will be sent to school—someday. To learn one thing at a time is better than trying to fill the mind with too much at once. For now you must be trained in the work to be done on the farm."

"But I could do both!" Mike insisted. "I'll work hard. I promise!"

"We will not talk again of schooling until you're used to your new home and duties," Mr. Friedrich said. Without another word he pushed back his chair and left the dining room. Mrs. Friedrich followed. Gunter paused only to smirk at Mike, then hurried to join his parents. Mike could hear the boards groan and snap under their weight as they started up the stairs.

Maybe Mr. Friedrich would change his mind if I told him that I can already read, and I won't need to spend too much time studying, Mike thought. He began to follow them, but stopped when he heard the low growl of Mr. Friedrich's whisper.

"Oh, no!" Mrs. Friedrich whimpered. "All these years you've been afraid they would send someone after you. Do you think that Reuben—"

"Quiet!" Mr. Friedrich snapped, and Mike slid back against the wall, melting into the shadows.

He slipped into the dining room and stood by the table, trying to piece together and understand all the strange facts he'd heard: Ulrich, the one who had died, had been a thief. For some reason Mike still didn't know,

Mr. Friedrich had been afraid for a long time that some-one would be sent after him. Mike's mind raced. There could be only one reason for this fear—Mr. Friedrich had murdered Ulrich. ✓

Horrified at his conclusion, Mike caught his breath. Now Mr. Friedrich suspected that Reuben was the one who was after him. Was it only because Reuben had spoken German? Was Reuben really after Mr. Friedrich? No, Mike told himself. Reuben just knew German poetry.

But Mike realized he had to talk to Reuben about Mr. Friedrich's suspicions. If Mr. Friedrich had killed one man—

Mike squared his shoulders. He was wasting time talking to himself. He had to help with the dishes and get himself to bed. He reached for a bowl but stopped as a deep yawn shuddered through his body.

Marta swung into the room and began to stack the plates. She took a look at Mike. "You're asleep on your feet," she said. "Go on to bed."

"I'll help you," Mike said, and he picked up the bread platter and the butter dish to carry to the kitchen.

"Hans Friedrich is a hard man," Marta said with a sigh, as she placed the dirty dishes on the table. "He should send you to school."

Mike looked up, surprised. "You heard?"

"There isn't much that Marta misses." Mike turned to see Reuben sitting in a chair in the dim light next to the fireplace.

"I like to know what goes on in this house," she said. "You'd know, too, if you could ever get your long nose out of that book." She shook her head in wonder as she turned to Mike. "Would you believe that Reuben reads while he's eating?"

"I can believe that," Mike said. "That's what I did with my book at home."

Marta studied him. "Do you really know how to read?"

"Yes," Mike said proudly. "Da and Frances taught me."

"Can you cipher?" Reuben asked. As Mike looked puzzled, Reuben explained, "Add and subtract figures."

"A little."

"Then perhaps while we work I can teach you some of the science of mathematics, besides giving you an introduction to the language of poetry." Reuben held up his worn poetry book as though it were a treasure.

Marta made a face. "If you're like me," she said to Mike, "you won't understand that poetry at all." Her eyes crinkled with laughter as she added in a conspiratorial tone, "I don't know why those poets couldn't just say what they had to say in plain words we could all understand."

Mike's answer didn't get out as his words were swallowed by another gigantic yawn.

"Go to bed," Marta said. "The day begins only too early around here, and you look more than ready for sleep."

"I'll bid you good night, too," Reuben said, and left the kitchen before Mike could warn him of anything.

The moment the door had closed behind Reuben, Mike said, "Marta, if you know what goes on in this house, then you must know why Mr. and Mrs. Friedrich are afraid."

Her eyes opened wide, and her lips parted as though she had something to say, but before she had the chance Mike asked, "Why would someone from Germany be sent after Mr. Friedrich? You know, don't you?"

Marta grasped Mike by the shoulders and held him tightly, her face so close to his he could feel her warm breath on his skin. "Never ask me such questions again! What happened in Germany is over! It is not something to talk about! And it is nothing for you to know!"

"Just tell me one thing." Mike was insistent. "You've

told me that you're not afraid of Mr. Friedrich, but that's not all the truth, is it?"

The despair on Marta's face was all the answer Mike needed. He pulled away and hurried up the stairs before she spoke.

In his room, with the door tightly closed, Mike raised the lower sash of his window, pulled off his shoes, and threw back the quilt on his bed. But when he saw what lay in his bed, he jumped back and clapped a hand over his mouth to stifle a cry. Sprawled in the middle of the bed was the hideous squashed body of a large pond frog.

Quickly, Mike shot a glance to each side, then stooped to look under the bed; Gunter was not in the small room, and there was nowhere else to hide. Mike gingerly picked up the ugly mess by the toes of one leg, carried it to the window, and tossed it outside.

Mike pulled the window down, scrubbed at his hands in the basin of water, and used the corner of his towel to rub at the place where the frog had lain. Everyone knew that if you touched a frog you could get warts. Just to be safe, he scrubbed his hands again.

Mike placed the towel over the spot and was so exhausted that he stumbled into bed. He tried to push the frog out of his mind. Stupid Gunter! Did he think he'd upset Mike for more than an instant with that sickening frog? Gunter wasn't even smart enough to come up with anything but dumb, childish tricks.

Mike tugged the puffy down quilt up to his ears, grudgingly admitting to himself that he had been caught again by one of those tricks. He shivered as he wondered, what would Gunter try next?

7

WHILE GUNTER WENT to school, Mike learned more about
farm work. Days passed quickly, and at night Mike col-
lapsed into bed after supper. On Saturday night the
high-backed iron tub was pulled into the kitchen in front
of the stove, and everyone took a bath in turn. On
Sunday Mike rode to church with the Friedrichs, and
Marta set off on foot toward her own church.

All this time, Mike kept a sharp eye on Gunter when-
ever he was nearby. He knew that at times Gunter spied
on him and Reuben, but there wasn't anything he could
do about it. He told Reuben about the conversations he
had overhead, but Reuben shook his head and reminded
him that an active imagination could cause Mike more
trouble than he'd bargained for. "The only German I
know is from Hölderlin's poetry and from some of my
mother's 'Old Country' expressions," Reuben added.

"Don't you see how Mr. Friedrich stares at you, with
his eyes all narrow and tight?" Mike demanded. "He acts

so strangely and suspiciously toward you, surely you must be aware of it."

"All I know about Mr. Friedrich is that he's a frugal, hardworking man," Reuben said. "And that's all I need to know. Whatever problems a man has are his own business and no one else's."

Mike ducked his head at the reprimand, but Reuben's attitude did nothing to lessen his fear of Mr. Friedrich.

Often Mike caught Gunter glaring at him through slitted eyes with such hatred that he stayed on guard, waiting for Gunter's next mean trick.

At the same time, Mike had to battle his own jealousy toward Gunter, who was sent to school in spite of his complaints that it was a waste of time, that the teacher didn't like him, and that Ezra, the youngest Blair boy, had knocked him down and bloodied his nose because he'd seen Gunter snitching a large slab of molasses cake from someone's dinner pail.

Gunter's lower lip curled down in a pout when he told the story. "I was just having fun. Ezra didn't give me a chance to explain."

"Those Blairs are a bad lot," Mr. Friedrich said. "Well, I hope you gave him as good as he gave you."

"I couldn't," Gunter muttered. "He's stronger, and the other boys were on his side."

"Oh, my poor Gunter," Mrs. Friedrich had said, sighing. "Maybe you should tell the teacher how those boys are bullying you."

At the time it was all Mike could do to keep from laughing aloud. The next morning, when he told Reuben the story as they worked to mend the fence in the high pasture, he did laugh, loudly and freely.

"Be careful of that Gunter," Reuben said. "It will make your life easier if you don't cross him."

"I'll be careful," Mike said. But at that moment nothing about Gunter could really worry him. The air was chill, but the sun was high and bright, and a sweet, sharp fragrance rose from the knee-deep golden grasses and clover. Bruna ran through the meadow, jumping and snapping at a bright butterfly.

Mike carefully helped to steady the support that Reuben had tightly wedged against the fence post while Reuben drove the post into place with heavy blows from a mallet. When they had finished, Mike stepped back and slowly turned to look out at the patches of forest and meadow, which lay before him in a gold and green patchwork.

"I wonder if this is anything like Ireland," he said. "Ma often said that Ireland was the most beautiful place on the earth, and I'm thinking that this place must be close to it."

Reuben wiped his sleeve across his forehead and smiled. "There's much in this world that's beautiful, Mike. I've heard there are mountains to the west that are higher than you can imagine, and rivers with water so clear you can see fish hiding on the bottom sands."

"Have you seen these things?" Mike asked.

"No, but they're there for the viewing."

"Will you go to those mountains and rivers someday?"

Reuben laughed. "I'll go back to my old and treacherous friend, the Missouri, which is sometimes so muddy that a few foolhardy souls have tried to walk on it."

Mike smiled. "I'd like to see the mountains. I'm going to travel farther west some day."

"Then do so," Reuben said. "*Wings have we—and as far as we can go we may find pleasure: wilderness and wood, blank ocean and mere sky, support that mood which with the lofty sanctifies the low.*"

"I understand the first part of that," Mike said. "Did your friend Shakespeare write it?"

"William Wordsworth did," Reuben told him. "He was also a poet of great renown."

"That's fine," Mike said. "They should have got along well, with both of them unable to put down words the way they come straight from the mouth."

"William Shakespeare lived many, many years ago, but William Wordsworth died just about the time that you were born."

"It's sorry I am, but I had nothing to do with it," Mike said. He grinned with mischief, and Reuben chuckled. "I like the poetry. I surely do," Mike said. "And someday maybe I'll understand it all. Tell again the part about the wings. I want to think about it."

The work went fast, and later that evening, after the cows had been put back into their stalls and the first stars were winking in the black sky, Reuben said, "We're through early tonight. You can take your time washing up for dinner."

Mike ran ahead, bouncing into the warm kitchen and smiling at Marta. "If you had wings," he asked, "would you fly to see the oceans and mountains?"

Marta's expression grew somber, and she sighed. "If I had wings," she said, "I think I would fly to see what Corey Blair was up to."

"Has he come back from the Kansas border?"

"I have no way of knowing." Marta shot an angry look in the direction of the parlor. "Mr. Friedrich ordered Corey not to set foot on this place."

Mike sidled toward the door as she spoke. Much as he liked Marta, he didn't want to hear any more about Corey.

He walked down the hallway, heading for the stairs, and had his foot on the bottom stair when he saw light flicker in his own room. As Mike drew back into the shadows the light went out, and someone hurried from Mike's room, quietly shutting the door. Mike hid under the staircase, peering out to see Gunter scrambling as fast as he could down the stairs.

59

The moment Gunter had disappeared in the direction of the parlor, Mike raced up the stairs and into his room. He picked up his lamp. Sure enough, the glass was warm to his touch. With fumbling fingers he lit the wick, then put the lamp down and studied his room.

Nothing seemed out of place. He had so few things, it was easy to keep track of them. He took off his coat, laid it across the chair, and stood by the bed, steeling himself for whatever dead animal Gunter might have hidden under the quilt.

Quickly Mike threw back the quilt and was surprised to discover that nothing horrible had been put in his bed. He decided that something must be under the bed. He tossed the quilt back into place, smoothed it out, and bent to peer under the bed. Nothing.

Mike straightened and tried to sort out the puzzle. Gunter had been in his room for a reason. He couldn't have taken anything, because Mike had nothing to take.

Carefully, he examined the chest, but could find nothing out of place. Whatever mean surprise Gunter had left behind, he'd hidden it well. But Mike would find it. He'd take the room apart, if need be. He had to discover what Gunter had been up to.

Mike gripped the edge of the straw-stuffed mattress to lift it from the rope slings on which it lay. As he did, his fingertips touched something cold and hard. Startled, he jumped back, then carefully eased up the mattress to see what was there.

Wedged between the rope and the wooden frame of the bed lay Mr. Friedrich's gold pocket watch!

As Mike stared at the watch, wondering what he was going to do, he heard heavy footsteps on the stairs and Gunter's raised voice. "I saw him take it, Papa! I saw Michael steal your watch!"

8

IF THE WATCH were found here in his room, Mike knew he'd be labeled a thief. Mr. Friedrich would send him back to New York where he'd surely go to prison! What could he do? His legs wobbling so they could barely hold him up, he squeezed his eyes shut, desperately searching for the answer. When he opened them again, he knew what he had to do.

Mike grabbed the watch, dropped the mattress down on the bed, smoothed the quilt into place, and threw open the door. He rushed out of the room and onto the stairs with such force that he crashed into Gunter. Gunter grabbed for the handrail to steady himself, and Mike stumbled, sitting down hard on the stairs.

Mr. Friedrich's large hand gripped the neck of Mike's shirt and roughly jerked him to his feet. "Get up!" he thundered.

"I didn't mean to be late to supper," Mike said.

"It's not suppertime we are concerned with." His

fingers dug into Mike's shoulder so hard that Mike cried out in pain.

Mrs. Friedrich appeared at the foot of the stairs. "What is it? What has happened?" she called and began to puff her way up the stairs.

"Michael tried to steal Papa's gold watch," Gunter announced.

"No! I didn't!" Mike cried.

"Yes, you did! I saw you!" Gunter turned so only Mike could see his face and smirked.

Marta ran up the stairs, squeezing to see around Mrs. Friedrich's shoulder. Reuben was right behind her.

Mike tried to squirm from Mr. Friedrich's grasp. "You're hurting my shoulder!" he cried.

"You will feel more pain than that before I am through with you!" Mr. Friedrich grunted.

"But I told you—I didn't steal your watch!"

"Tell me where you hid it," Mr. Friedrich demanded.

"I didn't!"

Gunter stepped forward. "I'll tell you, Papa. I saw him hide it under the mattress in his bed."

"Oh, my!" Mrs. Friedrich clapped her hands to her cheeks, her face pale with shock.

Marta gasped, her eyes wide with horror, but the expression on Reuben's face didn't change.

"That's not true!" Mike shouted.

"Isn't it? I'll show you," Gunter said. He led the way into Mike's room and lifted the edge of the mattress.

For a moment everyone just stared, until Gunter turned to Mike and furiously screeched, "Where is it? What did you do with it?"

"I told you!" Mike said. "I didn't take it!"

"It's got to be here!" Gunter tore the covers from the bed, then rummaged through the chest, but he came up empty-handed.

Mrs. Friedrich let out a long sigh of relief and said,

"The watch must be where it always is when Hans isn't wearing it—on the dresser in our room. Each night he carefully winds it and— "

"Be quiet, Irma!" Mr. Friedrich continued to scowl.

"I'll look!" Marta said and slipped from the room before anyone else could speak. In just a moment she returned, her right hand pressed to her chest as she tried to catch her breath, her words tumbling out in a rush. "The watch isn't where it should be!"

"Then where—"

Mr. Friedrich hadn't finished his question before Reuben stepped forward. "What is that bulge in your shirt pocket, Gunter?"

Surprised, Gunter clapped a hand over his pocket. Then he flushed a dark, mottled red. With all eyes on him he reached into the pocket and pulled out his father's watch.

"I didn't put it there!" he exploded. "Michael did! He must have found it and—" Gunter quickly started over. "He found it in Papa's room and put it in my pocket!"

"How could he do that?" Reuben asked. "Had you taken off your shirt and left it where Mike could get to it?"

"No," Gunter whined.

"I don't understand this at all," Mrs. Friedrich complained. She leaned back and fanned herself with her right hand.

Mike held his breath, hoping that none of them would understand how he'd made the switch.

"What were you doing with your papa's watch, Gunter?" his mother continued.

"Papa!" Gunter wailed. "Who are you going to believe—me, or Michael, who's a New York guttersnipe and a pickpocket?"

"I—I would believe my son," Mr. Friedrich grumbled,

but he let go of Mike's shoulder. Gratefully, Mike rubbed the sore spot.

"But Mike didn't have the watch. Gunter did," Marta said.

"This does not concern you. You will speak no more about it." Mr. Friedrich glared at Marta.

Reuben stepped forward. "I think it was just a boyish prank," he said.

"A boyish prank?" Mr. Friedrich began to bristle even more. "There is danger in allowing evil behavior to persist."

"*Wo aber Gefahr ist, wächst Das Retten da auch,*" Reuben said.

Mrs. Friedrich gasped, and for just an instant Mike saw terror in Mr. Friedrich's eyes. "What did you just say?" Mike whispered to Reuben.

Reuben must have seen the Friedrichs' fear, too. "It was just a line from a poem," he replied aloud. "It's translated as, 'But where danger is, grows also that which saves.' Mr. Friedrich is a churchgoing man. He'd understand that."

"I think I do understand," Mr. Friedrich said, so slowly and quietly that Mike's skin crawled. "You've never mentioned you speak German." Mike didn't understand what either of the two men were talking about.

Reuben quickly put an arm around Mike's shoulders and another around Gunter's and herded them toward the top of the stairs. "I know poetry. Now end this squabble," he said. "No one wants supper to get cold."

"Oh!" Marta cried. "The cream sauce will have scorched!" She squeezed past Reuben and raced down the stairs.

At the table Mike was on his best behavior and tried not to notice the sharp, angry looks both Mr. Friedrich and Gunter were giving him. But he had enough good, common sense—as Ma used to say—to know that Mr. Friedrich hadn't been satisfied with Reuben's answer. It was obvious that his suspicion of Reuben had grown even stronger. Mike also knew that Mr. Friedrich would hold this day against Mike, no matter that Mike had not been to blame. And Gunter would plot until he had planned something else to get Mike into such trouble that he'd be sent back to Tombs Prison.

For the first time since he'd arrived at the Friedrichs' farm, Mike had no appetite.

The next morning, as the last cow entered the pasture, Reuben called as usual, "Make sure the gate is securely fastened."

"I will," Mike answered. He dropped the bar, testing it to make sure that it was fitted tightly into place. He turned and saw Gunter standing near the barn, watching him. Gunter's lips twitched as though he were thinking of a secret joke before he turned and ran toward the road, swinging his covered lunch pail in one hand, his strapped books and slate in the other.

Mike hurried down to the barn to join Reuben, who had begun to clean the stalls. Mike quickly picked up the broom and got busy.

Reuben was silent while he worked. Occasionally Mike glanced at him from the corner of his eye, but he couldn't read the man's face. Was he angry at Mike, too? Surely he wouldn't believe that Mike had tried to steal Mr. Friedrich's watch! Reuben was his friend.

By the time they had finished the work in the barn, Mike was miserable with worry. Bluntly he faced Reuben and said, "I didn't take that watch. Don't you believe me?"

"Of course I believe you," Reuben said. "It wasn't hard to figure out what had happened. Gunter hid the watch in your room, you discovered the fact, and you slipped it into Gunter's pocket because there was nothing else you could do with it."

65

"That's right," Mike said. "That's exactly what happened." He sat on an overturned bucket and rested his chin in his hands. "Mr. Friedrich will probably figure out the last part. He won't believe that Gunter put the watch in my room. He'll just think I heard him coming and got rid of it the way any pickpocket would once his back was to the wall."

Reuben put a hand on Mike's shoulder. "As I told you before, Mike, you must be careful with Gunter. Be friendly toward the boy. I've seen you bristle around him like an angry rooster."

"He does his best to make me angry," Mike mumbled.

"That's no excuse," Reuben said. "Whether or not you give in to anger is your own choice."

"That's very like what Ma would be telling me." Mike stood and tried to smile, but the picture that came into his mind of Ma, with her arms wide, ready to enfold him, was so vivid that tears blurred his sight. "I miss Ma," he whispered. "I miss my family."

"Write to them," Reuben said. "That will make you feel better in itself, and when you get the answers to your letters, your world will brighten considerably."

"I've wanted to," Mike said, "but I have nothing to write with."

"Just ask Mr. Friedrich for some paper and the use of a quill pen and ink," Reuben said. "It would cost too little for him to begrudge you. He'll give them to you."

"Fine! I'll ask him tonight." Mike pulled back his shoulders. "What's the next job?"

"If you've got enough muscle for it, you can help me carry the buckets of feed to the hogs."

Mike didn't relish the job. Each time he'd done it, his arms had ached from the strain, but he said, "Sure. I'm ready. Those hogs will have their bellies—"

He was interrupted by Mrs. Friedrich calling, "Michael! Michael, where are you?"

66

Mike ran from the barn and toward the back porch stoop, where Mrs. Friedrich was standing, her shawl wrapped tightly around her.

"Ah," she said with satisfaction. "I knew you wouldn't be far from the house as yet. I need you to do something for me."

"Whatever you want, Mrs. Friedrich," Mike said.

She handed him a tightly woven reed basket. "Michael," she said, "will you please fill this with cockleburs? You'll find many in the wild grasses along the road."

Mike thought about the prickly burs that occasionally clung to the cuffs of his pants. "What would anyone want with cockleburs?" he blurted out.

"I am going to boil them with some alum," she said.

"Well, then, I suppose I'll be eating cockleburs and enjoying them," Mike said, "since anything you cook is the best eating there is in the whole state of Missouri."

Mrs. Friedrich laughed heartily. "Oh, Michael, you are so funny! I'm not going to cook them for us to eat. I'm going to make a green-yellow dye from them to dye the cloth for a new dress I'll make."

She went back into the house, still laughing, and Mike ran down the driveway to the road. He plucked at the prickly burs that hid among the grasses, now and then getting an extra harvest from the burs that clung to the legs of his trousers and the fingers of his gloves. The basket was large, and Mike found himself far down the road before it was even half-filled. As he stopped to stretch his arms and arch his tired back, he realized that he had traveled quite a distance. The Friedrich farm buildings were no longer in sight. Far down the hill, in the opposite direction, he could see another white house with smoke rising from its chimney. He wondered who lived there.

Mike bent once more to his task, eager to finish, but

67

straightened when he heard the dull pounding of a horse's hooves on the road. He watched a rider from down the hill come closer and saw that it was Corey Blair.

Corey reined his speckled gray horse near where Mike was standing and said, "You're the new boy at the Friedrich place."

Mike nodded. "I'm Mike Kelly."

"And I'm Corey Blair. We heard some tales about you, Mike."

Mike's backbone stiffened, and he pulled back his shoulders, but Corey chuckled and said, "I'd a' liked to seen you tangle with that outlaw on the train."

Corey swung from his horse, holding the reins loosely, and said, "I don't hold a man's past agin' him, Mike. In fact, I figger you and me could become friends."

"Thanks," Mike said. "I'd like that. The more friends I have, the better."

"You was there when Mr. Friedrich throwed me out of his house," Corey said. "He hadn't no right to do that."

"He gets angry a lot," Mike said. "I think he was angry that you were going to fight on the side of slavery."

"A man's got a right to his own opinions," Corey said.

Mike was puzzled. Corey seemed open and friendly. How could somebody like that believe in slavery? "Do you really think that people should have slaves?" Mike asked him.

In turn, Corey looked as though he couldn't understand Mike. "There's nothin' to think about," he said. "Facts are that Missouri is a slave state and nobody's got a right to change that, 'ceptin' our own lawmakers. Most of all, we don't need some Yankees comin' in to tell us what to do." He shoved his hat back over his roughly cut, sun-bleached hair and proudly added, "My grandpap helped settle Missouri, and Missouri people decide for theirselves what they want."

68

"Then shouldn't the Kansas people decide what they want?" Mike asked.

"You know any of them Kansas people?" Corey asked. When Mike shook his head, Corey said, "I didn't think so. A bunch of them are every bit as crazy as that old John Brown who got hisself hung last year. You know about John Brown?"

"No."

"Well, Brown—along with his sons and some other folks—in the middle of the night come and drug some good old Missouri farm folk out of their beds and murdered them and stole their belongings and said they was doin' it to stop slavery. This feller Brown went on causin' a heap of trouble, all in the name of freein' some slaves, who—if they knew what was best for them—probably didn't even want to be freed. Well, anyhow, after Brown's raiders caused a lot more trouble, even takin' over a U.S. Government arsenal, a lot more folks got killed. Old Brown was tried and hung. And everybody would'a been better off if he'd never started nothin' in the first place."

"Then why did you go to the border to fight?" Mike asked.

"Because I got to," Corey said. "Weren't you payin' attention?"

This discussion was getting nowhere, Mike thought, so he deliberately changed the subject. "Marta's been in a bad mood ever since Mr. Friedrich told you to leave the house."

Corey looked pleased. "She missed me?"

"I guess."

Corey took a step closer to Mike and bent forward, lowering his voice. "You and me could help each other out, Mike."

"How?" Mike was wary.

"Well, for one thing, since I can't go near the Friedrich

69

place with Old Man Friedrich there, I can't tell Marta that I'm back home again."

"Oh," Mike said. "Is that what you want? Sure, I'll be glad to tell her. Yesterday she was wondering where you were."

Corey, a broad smile on his face, stuck a hand into his coat pocket and took out a folded square of paper. "I want a little more than that. I want you to take her this note from me."

Mike hesitated, but Corey urged, "Just slip it to her when no one else is around. You ain't gonna get into any trouble."

He reached into his pocket again and came up with a half dozen pennies. "I'll give you this for takin' the trouble. It's no secret that Friedrich is stingy with his money, so I doubt he'll be handin' out treats when you're in town. This is enough to get you a good-sized paper twist of candy drops."

It didn't take Mike long to decide. How could he get into trouble just slipping Marta a small piece of paper? And the pennies were tempting. "All right," he said. "I'll do it."

"If there's an answer," Corey said, "just find your way back here. Either me or one of my brothers will spy you from our place." He smiled. "There'll be more pennies for you each time you do me this favor."

"Thanks," Mike said and grinned at Corey. "Glad to oblige."

Mike pocketed the note and tied the pennies into a corner of his handkerchief. Then he worked at a feverish pace to fill the basket. Eventually it was full. He ran back to the house, out of breath as he thumped the basket onto the kitchen table.

"Very good," Mrs. Friedrich said. "That was fast work!" She reached into a deep ceramic crock and pulled out a fat biscuit. She split it, buttered it, and tucked a thick slab of cold meat into it. "Here is a little treat for you. Sit—over there at the table by the window. Eat it before you go back to work." By the time Mike sat down, she had put a large glass of milk in front of him, too.

Mike wolfed down the biscuit and milk. Working outdoors made him awfully hungry. He carried the empty glass to Marta, who was busy scraping carrots at the other table.

"Here, give that to me," she said impatiently. She grabbed the glass but stopped and blinked with surprise as the note was thrust into her other hand.

Mike put one finger to his lips. Marta smiled, her cheeks suddenly turning bright pink, and shoved the note into the pocket of her apron.

"Reuben is clearing the last stalks from the corn-field," Marta told Mike. "It would be a good idea for you to lend him a hand."

Mike worked beside Reuben with a fierce energy. Occasionally he whistled or hummed a lively tune. He had coins in his pocket, with the promise of more to come, and Marta would be back to her own good nature again. The day had turned out to be much better than he had thought.

By dinnertime his stomach rumbled with hunger, and he was glad to hear the bell clanging loudly. He wondered how he had once survived on those meager meals of potatoes and cabbage.

Reuben put down his hoe and smiled at Mike. "I'm glad to see your spirits have improved so quickly."

"That they have," Mike said. They briskly strode toward the house and both dogs ran to meet them. "While I was out on the roadside Corey Blair came by."

"So he's back, is he?" Reuben said. "*On, ye brave, who rush to glory, or the grave.*"

"Corey's brave enough, I guess," Mike answered, "but

71

in my opinion there's little glory in what he's doing. It's my belief that no one should be a slave."

"Good for you," Reuben said and looked pleased.

"I don't understand why people think slavery is right."

"The answer is that they *don't* think. If they examined the issue, they might have to act on it, so it's easier for them not to think at all."

Mike reached down to scratch Wulf behind the ears. "At least now that Corey's back, we can count on a great improvement in Marta's disposition."

Reuben laughed, and Mike continued. "He gave me a note to slip to her."

Reuben's laugh broke off. "You're in no position to take extra chances, Mike. Let Corey work out another way to communicate with Marta, if he must."

Mike shrugged. "No one saw me give it to her. There's nothing to fear."

They had reached the back stoop, so Reuben didn't answer. Instead they splashed their faces and forearms in the basin of water, rubbed with soap until their skin was red, then dried with the linen towel that hung on a nail.

Mike left Reuben in the kitchen and hurried into the dining room, where he managed to slide into his chair just as Mr. and Mrs. Friedrich were sitting down.

As soon as the blessing was over, Mike asked, "Mr. Friedrich, could I please have some paper and the use of your pen and ink bottle, so I could write to my mother and to my brothers and sisters?"

Mr. Friedrich paused in his job of scooping mashed and buttered yellow squash onto the plate in his left hand. He seemed to give Mike's question long and serious thought. Mrs. Friedrich twisted her fingers together nervously, waiting for his answer, and Marta shifted from one foot to the other with impatience.

Finally Mr. Friedrich said, "Mind you, I approve of

your industrious spirit and have no reason to deny you writing paper. "But ..."

Mike held his breath. He'd had no idea Mr. Friedrich would do anything but agree.

"But there is a problem, Michael. The postage on those letters would cost money, and so far the work you have done has not been enough to begin to make up to us the generous room and board we have given you. Now you are asking me to spend hard-earned money on postage for your letters."

Mike slumped back in his chair, so disappointed he felt ill. "I've never sent a letter to anyone. I didn't think of the cost."

"Three cents a letter is little to spend," Marta muttered.

Mr. Friedrich threw her a quick, angry look before turning back to Mike.

But Mike had perked up at Marta's words. "If it's just three cents, then I could pay some of the postage!" He fumbled with the handkerchief he tugged from his pocket and pulled out the coins that Corey had given him. "Here!" he said. "This would be enough for two letters!"

Mr. Friedrich stared at the coins. Then he raised his head and thundered at Mike, "Where did you get that money?"

9

WHAT HAD HE done! As the blood drained from Mike's face he clutched the edge of the table for support and struggled to keep a large, black spot from swallowing him. Wild excuses swirled through his head like leaves in a wind, and he was unable to snatch even one that could be of any use.

"You heard my question," Mr. Friedrich demanded. "Where did you get those pennies?"

Marta stepped forward. "Michael did me a favor, and I repaid him." She spoke firmly, but Mike wondered if anyone besides himself could hear the slight tremor in her voice.

"You have coins to spare?" Mr. Friedrich scowled up at her.

Marta had regained all of her usual spirit. "With such a large house to care for, and no other serving girl to help Mrs. Friedrich and me with the work, there are many times when I would gladly part with a cent or two to gain another pair of hands."

"Michael has outdoor work to do."

Marta didn't give him a chance to continue. "And who's to say this work was not out-of-doors? Why, only this morning Michael was sent to gather a basket of cockleburs so we could make dye for the new cloth. And even so—"

"That's enough! While you talk incessantly the food gets cold." Mr. Friedrich finished his job of filling the plate in his hands, studied it, and grunted, "Give this to Mrs. Friedrich."

"Yes, sir," Marta said. She carefully took the plate to her mistress, then walked briskly to the kitchen door. But before leaving the room she paused and turned to Mike. "If you need more coins to pay for letters to your family, Michael, I'll have them for you. One favor deserves another."

"Thank you," Mike mumbled, awed at her bravery in the face of Mr. Friedrich's obvious displeasure. He'd be glad to carry messages for Marta anytime, after the way she had saved him from his own thoughtless mistake.

Mike poked at the food on the plate Mr. Friedrich handed him, unable to choke down more than a few bites. His stomach still churned from fear, and it was all he could do to keep his hands from trembling.

"Michael, you're not eating. Are you not well?" Mrs. Friedrich asked.

"My stomach hurts," Mike said truthfully.

Mrs. Friedrich reached out to lay a hand on his forehead. "Hans," she said, "Michael's skin is cold and damp."

Mr. Friedrich stretched his mouth around another huge forkful of food and didn't bother to look up from his plate.

Mrs. Friedrich turned back to Mike. "Are you having chills?"

Mike shivered, but he didn't know if it was Mrs.

Friedrich's suggestion or remnants of fear that caused it. "I *am* cold," he whispered.

She pushed back her chair. "Then we will give you a cup of hot tea with honey and tuck you in bed."

At this Mr. Friedrich raised his head and stared at Mike. "Nonsense," he said. "The boy needs to get back to work. The outdoor air will do more for him than tea and bed, which is something only a woman would think of."

"But, Hans," Mrs. Friedrich said, "last summer, when you came down with chills and fever, you let me feed you herb tea and put you to bed. You even asked for an extra quilt."

Mr. Friedrich leaned toward his wife and glowered. "We are not discussing me. We are discussing a lazy boy."

Mrs. Friedrich clutched her hands together as she quietly explained, "The chillblains could go into consumption, and Michael could die, and how would we explain that to the committee?"

Mike's eyes widened in horror, and he shivered again.

For just an instant Mr. Friedrich hesitated, but he studied Mike carefully and said, "He doesn't look that ill to me."

"But, Hans . . ."

Mike couldn't let Mrs. Friedrich keep defending him. Mr. Friedrich would only get angry with her, too. So he spoke up quickly. "Thank you, Mrs. Friedrich, but I think some fresh air might be just what I need." He placed his napkin on the table next to his plate. "May I go outside now, Mr. Friedrich?"

"Yes. Yes, go." Mr. Friedrich's gaze was puzzled. "If Reuben has not finished his meal, then you can collect eggs for Marta."

Mike hurried into the kitchen where Marta grabbed him around the neck and practically stuffed him into his

76

coat. "Thank you for helping me," Mike mumbled as he struggled to get free.

"As I said, one good turn deserves another," she answered, pressing a folded piece of paper into his hand. "Take this to the road. Run! It's my answer to Corey."

"But the eggs—"

"I've already gathered them from the coop. Go! Hurry!"

Reuben pushed back his chair and got to his feet. "I don't think this is a wise thing to do," he began.

But Marta simply shook her apron at him, as she would at an arrogant rooster, and gave Mike a push. "Run, Mike!" she hissed.

Mike did. When he arrived at the place in the road where he could be seen from the Blair house, he was so out of breath that he leaned over, arms braced against his thighs, and loudly gulped for air.

"Haloo!" The voice was so close to him that Mike straightened up with a yelp. A boy who was tanned almost the color of his brown hair grinned at Mike and staggered the last few steps toward him, his hand on his chest as he drew in long breaths.

"I'm Ezra. Corey sent me," the boy managed to say between gasps.

"You're the one who knocked Gunter down at school?" Mike grinned back. As the thought struck him, he whirled to look behind him. "Is school out already?"

"Naw," Ezra said. "I'm stayin' home a couple'a days to help with the hog butcherin'." He paused, managing to breathe normally again. "You ever seen that done?"

Mike shook his head, and Ezra made a face. "You'll find out what it's like soon enough. We heard Old Man Friedrich's workin' you hard as an old mule. How can you stand livin' with those Friedrichs?"

"Mrs. Friedrich's nice enough," Mike said. "And Marta and Reuben."

"Marta," Ezra said, as though he'd just remembered. "You got a note from her to Corey?"

"Right here." Mike handed over the folded paper.

"I hope Corey don't get it into his head to marry her," Ezra said. "Except for Ma, we only got men and boys in our family, and I'd sure hate to see a girl move in."

Mike gave a wry smile. "Mr. Friedrich's doing his best to help you there."

Ezra chuckled. "I gotta hurry back, or Corey will skin my hide along with the hogs'. If you can ever get away from Old Man Friedrich for some time of your own, come on by the house."

"Thanks," Mike said. He reluctantly watched Ezra run down the hill. He'd like to have Ezra for a friend. But when would he have any time to spend with a friend? Mr. Friedrich would never allow it—especially if his friend were a Blair. Mike turned and raced toward the house, hushing Bruna and Wulf, who had run to greet him. He reached the side yard just as Reuben came out of the kitchen door.

Reuben gave him one quick look and said, "Better splash cold water on your face. Running has made it flushed."

Mike had no sooner started toward the bench, with its pan of cold water, than Mr. Friedrich stepped outside, Mrs. Friedrich right behind him.

"Ach! Will you look at the boy!" she cried. "So much for your fresh air. See how his face is red and feverish."

"I'm all right," Mike said, but Mrs. Friedrich scrambled down the steps of the back stoop and wrapped her arms around him. "Hans," she said, "Michael needs rest."

"And tea with honey." Mr. Friedrich's voice was sarcastic.

But Mrs. Friedrich didn't seem to notice. "Of course. Tea with honey," she echoed.

78

"Mrs. Friedrich," Mike tried to say, but his face was muffled against her apron.

"Very well," Mr. Friedrich said, "but he had better be well by tomorrow morning, because there is much work that will need to be done."

He turned toward Reuben, shouting in his frustration, "Why are you standing there, always watching me, always prying and snooping? Must you poke your long nose into conversations that do not concern you, like a woman?"

"I won't have you use a tone like that to me. Never speak to me in that way again," Reuben said, his voice so filled with controlled anger that it was more frightening than Mr. Friedrich's loud shouting.

Mike twisted around Mrs. Friedrich, who was leading him up the steps, to look at Reuben, whose face was pale, and whose eyes glittered like sharp stones.

"I can talk to you any way I like. You are only the hired hand, or at least that is what we are pretending, isn't it? Isn't it!" Mr. Friedrich demanded.

The door shut behind them, so Mike couldn't hear Reuben's answer. Although he was glad Reuben had stood up to Mr. Friedrich, he was also frightened. Why had Mr. Friedrich accused Reuben of prying? What did he think Reuben was going to find?

"Up to bed with you," Mrs. Friedrich said. "I'll make some tea and bring it to you in just a few minutes. No dawdling." She couldn't keep her voice from trembling.

Up in his room, Mike quickly pulled off his boots and clothes and put on the nightshirt he'd received the day he and his brothers and sisters had set off on the orphan train. The Children's Aid Society had given them each a few things. He sat on the edge of the bed, trying to sort out all the mixed-up things that had happened to him today. He had every intention of leading a good, honest life, but now he was acting as a secret messenger between Marta and Corey, using every trick he knew to keep Gunter from causing trouble for him, and—through no fault of his own—pretending to be ill! He put his head into his hands and groaned aloud.

"Ach, poor *liebchen*," Mrs. Friedrich said from the doorway. There was color in her face again, and her hands were steady as she held out a cup and saucer to Mike. "Here—drink this tea, as hot as you can stand it."

She waited while Mike sipped at the tea. It wasn't half bad, with its smell of peppermint and spicy flowers, and the honey she had stirred in was thick on his tongue. In just a few minutes he had gulped it down.

"Mrs. Friedrich," he said, "I don't understand some of the things Mr. Friedrich said to Reuben. Why did he tell him that—"

Mrs. Friedrich clapped a hand over Mike's mouth. "Hush! We cannot talk of this." She took her hand away and whispered, "Please forget what Hans told Reuben. He was upset. He did not mean what he said."

"But—"

For an instant she closed her eyes and gave a long, shuddering sigh. When she spoke, it was as though she had forgotten Mike was in the room. "I am so tired of being afraid," she murmured. "We have worked very hard here to build what we have for ourselves and for Gunter. I cannot leave it. I cannot run again."

Mike knew better than to say a word. He sat without moving, almost afraid to breathe, until Mrs. Friedrich suddenly pulled herself back to the present and became aware of him.

"You have drunk the tea. Good, good." She tucked the quilt around him as he lay back on the bed. "Sleep now," she said. "Sometimes sleep is the best medicine." Quietly she tiptoed from the room and shut the door.

Sleep? With all he had to think about? But the bed was warm and cozy, and Mike snuggled into it.

80

The next thing he knew the room was dark, and his door was slowly opening, an inch at a time.

Mike sat up in bed, calling, "Who's there?"

The door opened wide, and Mrs. Friedrich stepped inside the room. She lit Mike's lamp from the one in her hand. "How are you feeling?" she asked.

Mike didn't have to think for long. "Hungry," he said.

Her cheeks sagged, but she managed a wisp of a smile. "Good. I knew the rest would make you feel better."

"Thank you, Mrs. Friedrich," Mike said. "I'll get up and help Marta put the supper on the table."

"Supper was over an hour ago." This time her smile was stronger. "You should see your face, Michael. You look like a small dog out in the rain. Did you think I would let you go hungry?" She patted the lump in the quilt that covered Mike's feet. "You stay in bed. In just a few minutes I'll bring you some hot bean and ham soup and some corn bread I saved for you. A little butter and honey on the bread should taste nice."

Mike lay back with a contented sigh.

At the door she paused. "If you feel strong enough after you have eaten, you can write to your mother and your brothers and sisters. There are paper, a quill pen, ink, and wipers on top of the chest. Oh—and a slate for your lap on which you can put the paper when you write."

"Thank you!" Mike beamed.

Still Mrs. Friedrich didn't leave. She looked at the dark window, the floor, and finally at Mike. "I hope you will tell your family the good things about your life with us."

"The good things? Like your delicious meals?" Mike asked.

She brightened. "Yah! Maybe tell them about the

81

rolling hills and the trees with their red and golden leaves."

Mike realized what she was trying to tell him. "Will Mr. Friedrich read my letters before they're mailed?"

"He says of course he must," she murmured, as though she were repeating her husband's words. "He has the great responsibility of teaching and training you for a better life than the one you had."

"I understand," Mike answered.

Mrs. Friedrich hurried through the door, and Mike could hear the stair boards creak and snap. At first he let anger simmer under his skin the way the hot tea had simmered in the heavy cup. Mr. Friedrich had no right to read his letters, to decide what Mike could or couldn't say!

But anger slid away as he admitted to himself that even without Mrs. Friedrich's warning, he would not have told Ma or the others about the way Gunter and Mr. Friedrich treated him. What could any of them do about it? Nothing! They had enough problems of their own. He hugged the quilt to his chin, and his chest ached as he thought of Danny and Peg and Megan and Petey and Frances Mary. He hoped with all his heart that their homes had turned out to be happier than this one. "Oh, Ma!" he whispered and once more fought back the tears.

In a few minutes Mrs. Friedrich brought the supper tray. Mike ate gratefully. Then, still in his nightshirt, he sat at the end of the bed next to the chest and carefully wrote his letters. First he wrote to Ma. He wrote about the good food, about the golden meadows and green forests, and about the animals on the farm.

Then he hesitated. He wanted to write that he would live with the Friedrichs only as long as he had to, and that when he was old enough he would head farther west in search of mountains and rivers and lakes and plains and all the other wondrous things he imagined from the stories Reuben told.

"That's Michael Kelly!" someone would whisper as he rode on horseback through a dusty western town. "Kelly's traveled to the tops of the mountain peaks, from ocean to ocean, and into wild country where no one has ever dared to set foot." And men would respectfully move aside and touch the brims of their hats to him.

But he wrote only, "Your loving son, Michael." His letters to his brothers and sisters were very much the same.

Mike wiped the pen point carefully and tightened the top on the bottle of ink before he placed them beside his letters. The house was quiet. He was probably the only one still awake. He snuffed out the wick in his lamp and climbed back into bed, huddling into a ball as he waited for his own body to warm the bed. There was so much to think about, so many questions that needed answering. He could hardly wait to talk with Reuben in the morning.

When morning came, Mike woke with a start. "Hurry!" Mr. Friedrich shouted as he hammered on the door to Mike's room. Although this early morning commotion took place every day, Mike still found it hard to get used to.

As he dressed he glanced out his window. Lantern light gleamed through the open doors; Reuben had already begun the milking. Mike wondered what time Reuben woke up every morning and how he managed it without Mr. Friedrich to shout at him.

When Mike went down to breakfast, he took his stack of letters with him and laid them next to Mr. Friedrich's plate.

Mr. Friedrich looked at the letters suspiciously, then picked up the one on the top, opened it, and read it.

Mike held his breath, but Mr. Friedrich only nodded, tossed the paper down again, and said, "There's no hurry for me to read these. They can't be mailed until we go to town next week."

"I wrote their addresses on the back," Mike said.

"I'll give you envelopes for the letters—if they pass my inspection," Mr. Friedrich said. He paused. "And you can give me your coins. Since the postage for all these letters will cost more than you have, I will pay it and expect you to perform extra chores to reimburse me."

Mike nodded reluctantly. He'd be getting more pennies from Corey, but there'd be no way he could let Mr. Friedrich know about them.

The morning blessing was always a short one, and the meal was eaten in haste, since the cows needed to be milked and all the animals fed.

Mike pulled on his coat and hurried outside. It was Saturday, and there was no school, so Gunter would be home all day. Even though Gunter had his own chores to do, Mike was sure that he would find enough time to think up something to get Mike into trouble. He'd have to keep his eyes open and his wits about him.

"I see you're feeling better now," Reuben said, as Mike entered the barn.

He smiled, and Mike was immediately cheered. He had worried that Reuben would be angry with him for missing Friday afternoon's work.

Mike glanced around to make sure that Gunter was not nearby and lowered his voice. "I don't understand the things that Mr. Friedrich said to you."

"Nor do I," Reuben answered.

"Did you ask him what he meant when he said you were pretending to be his hired hand?"

"I asked for no explanations," Reuben said. "The man was so angry, he wasn't rational."

"Mrs. Friedrich is afraid of something—something

84

besides her husband," Mike said. "Last night she said she didn't want to run away again."

"Mike," Reuben said, "the Friedrichs' problems are their own business and not our concern."

"But maybe they do concern you. I've heard them whispering about you."

For a moment Reuben frowned. Then he released the nearest cow from her stall and said, "I learned long ago to avoid others' petty quarrels and angers. Let's get these ladies out to pasture. Where are the dogs?"

Mike ran ahead, whistling for Bruna and Wulf, who were already running toward the barn. He opened the gate and hung on it as the cows slowly marched through. The early air was fragrant with the sharp scent of the meadow grasses, and the sky was ribboned with streaks of pink and gold. It was a beautiful day, and for the moment Mike convinced himself that Reuben was right. Worrying about the Friedrichs was a waste of good time.

As the last cow walked through, Mike avoided her switching tail and swung the gate shut, checking to make sure it was carefully fastened.

Mike began to run back down the hill to the barn, but Gunter called to him. "Marta wants more wood carried to the house."

Before Mike could answer, Gunter disappeared around the corner of the barn, so Mike added more wood to the bin by the back stoop, even though there seemed to be plenty on hand.

As Mike ran into the barn, Reuben rested on his shovel and asked, "What kept you?"

"I had to put more wood in the bin."

"There should have been plenty," Reuben said.

Mike shrugged. "That's what I thought, but Marta wanted more." He picked up the broom and energetically set to work cleaning the stalls.

He had just finished when Mr. Friedrich stomped into

the barn and reached for the leather harness. "We will take the mules to the north field and work together to clear it," he said. He ignored Reuben and turned his scowl on Mike. "And I will tolerate no laziness."

"No, sir," Mike stammered. He saw Gunter sidle into the barn behind his father. Gunter glanced at Mike and smiled a strange, secret smile before he quickly looked away.

Mike immediately became busy following Mr. Friedrich's orders and put Gunter out of his mind. Soon the mules were in harness.

To the noisy jangling of the harness and the snorting and blowing of the mules, Mr. Friedrich, Gunter, Reuben, and Mike left the barn and headed up the road toward the north field, the dogs racing ahead.

No one spoke until Gunter, who walked next to his father, called to Mike, "What were you doing at the pasture?"

"Taking the cows to pasture, the way I always do," Mike answered.

"I mean later—just before we harnessed the mules."

"I wasn't at the pasture then," Mike said.

"Yes, you were," Gunter insisted. "I saw you. You were running from the pasture."

"I was not!"

"Was too!"

Mr. Friedrich's hand was rough on Mike's shoulder. "Enough of this," he said and gave Mike a shake hard enough to make him stumble. "Keep your mind on your work, and you will have no time for foolish arguments."

Reuben led the mules into the field, and the others followed. The mules were hitched to a contraption with a row of sharp-toothed metal disks.

"What is that?" Mike asked.

"It's a harrow, and it's used to break up the soil," Reuben said.

86

"Don't waste time with explanations," Mr. Friedrich grumbled and began to snap out directions. "You boys, run ahead and look for stones. When you see them, carry them quickly to pile at the side here. The stones can break the disks."

The four of them set to work. It didn't surprise Mike that Gunter let him do most of the stooping and carrying. They had worked for only an hour or so when the bell at the house began clanging. Mr. Friedrich pulled the mules to a stop and wiped an arm across his forehead. "It's not noon," he said. "It's not time to stop for our meal."

As the clanging continued, Reuben was the first to react. "Something's wrong!" he cried. He quickly secured the mules' lead to the nearest fence post and ran in the direction of the house, almost as fast as Wulf and Bruna.

Mike raced after Reuben. Mr. Friedrich and Gunter puffed behind him.

As they crested the hill, Mike could see two men on horseback who were herding cattle up the road toward the pasture. The gate to the pasture stood wide open.

"The cattle!" Mr. Friedrich wheezed. "Those are my cattle! What are they doing on the road? How did they get out?"

Gunter grabbed his father's arm and shook it. "That's why Mike was at the pasture!" he cried. "He deliberately opened the gate! Papa, Mike let your cattle out!"

10

MR. FRIEDRICH DIDN'T even look at Mike. He ran after the horsemen, who were driving the cattle into the pasture with the help of the dogs. He carefully closed and fastened the gate, then turned to the men.

"Corey Blair!" he stammered. His face was deep red with anger.

"Oh, Hans, don't be angry! Corey was helping!" Mrs. Friedrich's hands fluttered to her face as she called from the stoop where she and Marta stood. Mike saw her shrink back as Mr. Friedrich frowned, then turned away.

"Your cattle was out on the road," Corey said. "Me and my brother brought 'em back for you."

"For this I thank you," Mr. Friedrich muttered. He began to stride toward Mike and Gunter, but Corey swung from his horse and stood in his way.

"Mr. Friedrich," Corey said, "we're neighbors. There's no call for us not to act neighborly, is there?"

Mr. Friedrich folded his arms across his chest and

glared at Corey. "I have already thanked you. Is there more that you want?"

"Yes," Corey said. He glanced in Marta's direction, then smiled easily, as though Mr. Friedrich's bad temper didn't bother him at all. "I'd like your permission for me to come calling on Marta. Will you give it?"

"No! I will not! Marta is not ready for marriage."

Corey shook his head. "She's over the age that most of the women around here marry at. Healthy, strong, good-lookin' woman like Marta shoulda been married long ago."

"She was."

"Huh?" Corey took a step backward.

"She should have told you. She was widowed when she was seventeen. She has been under our protection ever since." Mr. Friedrich stepped so close to Corey that Corey had to back away to keep from being butted by Mr. Friedrich's round stomach. "If Marta marries again it will be to a hardworking, sensible German, not to a young fool who would rather fight than work."

Corey's face flushed almost as dark as Mr. Friedrich's. "I'm a hard worker. You can take a look at our place. We all work hard."

Mr. Friedrich waved Corey aside and walked quickly to where Mike, Gunter, and Reuben were standing. "Time is valuable, and you are stealing mine. I've thanked you. Now be gone with you."

"I ain't stealin' anythin' that's yours!" Corey exploded. "I done you a favor, and small reward I got for it!"

Mr. Friedrich ignored Corey and kept walking toward the north field. Corey tugged his hat down firmly and swung up on his horse's back. Without another word he and his brother galloped toward the Blairs' farm.

Reuben, with a worried glance at Mike, strode after Mr. Friedrich, while Gunter smirked and ran to catch up with his father. Mike, his legs shaking so much it was hard to walk, hurried after them. As soon as the Blairs had disappeared down the road, Gunter called, "Papa, it's all Mike's fault! He let the cattle out on purpose!"

Terrified, Mike cried, "I didn't! I wouldn't do a thing like that. I know those are prize cattle."

Mr. Friedrich stopped, turned, and glared at Mike. "We have work that must be done," he said. "We will not talk of this matter until tonight."

"You're going to beat him, Papa, aren't you?" Gunter asked.

Mike gasped, but Gunter continued, "And send him back to New York, where he belongs!"

"Get to work, both of you," Mr. Friedrich ordered. He reached for the mules' lead, and Mike ran, stumbling over the broken earth, to the spot where he had been removing stones when the bell had rung. He worked without stopping until Marta rang the bell to call them to dinner.

When Mr. Friedrich bowed his head for the blessing and loudly prayed for guidance in his treatment of Michael, Mike slumped in his chair. His hands and feet were numb, and chills shook his backbone as Mr. Friedrich wondered aloud as to the wisdom of keeping a boy who continued his evil ways without a shred of repentance.

Over and over Mike thought, *He can't send me back! Not to Tombs Prison! He can't!* The food could have been boiled hay, for all Mike knew. He was so frightened he could barely taste or swallow.

After dinner the four returned to the north field and worked until the sun had disappeared behind the western hills. It was dark by the time the cows were brought back to the barn, so they fed and cared for the animals by lantern light. Mike ached with exhaustion as he stumbled toward the basin of water at the back stoop and shed his gloves and coat.

As Mike reached for the lump of lye soap, Mr. Friedrich's hand clamped on his shoulder and pulled him back. "We have something to talk about," he said. "I have made my decision."

Reuben and Gunter turned, their eyes on Mr. Friedrich. Mike could see that Reuben was wary, but Gunter's expression was gleeful. Mr. Friedrich waved an impatient hand at them and said, "Wash quickly and go inside. This has nothing to do with either of you."

Gunter began to splash noisily, but Reuben said, "Mike is just a boy."

"Who is in *my* care, not yours!" Mr. Friedrich interrupted. "You heard me—go inside!"

Mike took a deep breath and tried to stand as tall as he could, even though Mr. Friedrich's hand was like a heavy weight pushing him down. "Mr. Friedrich, I did *not* open the gate to let your cattle out."

"Don't lie. It only makes your offense worse."

"I'm not lying. I'm telling the truth."

"Gunter saw you at the pasture when you should not have been there."

"That's right," Gunter said.

"I wasn't at the pasture. I was filling the wood bin for Marta. Gunter told me she asked for more wood."

"We will see about that," Mr. Friedrich said. He bellowed, "Marta!" so loudly that Mike winced.

The door flew open, and Marta, still wrapping a shawl around her shoulders, poked her head outside. "What is the matter? What do you want?" she asked.

"The answer to a question," Mr. Friedrich said. "This morning, did you tell Gunter that more wood was needed here in the bin?"

She looked puzzled. "No," she said. "There was plenty of wood in the bin. Mike filled it yesterday evening."

"But Gunter said—" Mike began.

"That's enough," Mr. Friedrich snapped. "All of you—go

inside the house." He whirled, nearly dragging Mike off his feet, and marched rapidly back to the barn. In the lantern light his shadow swept ahead like a monstrous giant.

Inside the barn, Mr. Friedrich put down the lantern and studied Mike. "I have decided not to send you back to New York, Michael. I have accepted the responsibility of teaching you to live a good, moral life, but you are making my task a difficult one. It is hard for me to understand why you cannot see the evil of your ways."

"I'm not evil!" Mike cried. He winced as Mr. Friedrich's fingertips dug into his shoulder, but anger gave him the courage he needed to continue. "Let me tell you what happened—why the cattle were let out of the pasture."

"Very well. I will listen. I pride myself on being a just man."

Mike had a different opinion about that, but he was desperate for a chance to explain. "Gunter wants you to send me back to New York. He made up that story about Marta wanting extra wood in the bin so that I'd be away from my regular chores without an excuse. And he also lied about seeing me at the pasture, because he's the one who unlatched the gate so the cattle could get out."

"You are calling my son a liar?" Mr. Friedrich's face darkened with fury, and he puffed up like a fat rooster ready to fight.

"I'm telling only the truth," Mike said.

His hand still clenching Mike's shoulder, Mr. Friedrich reached to a nail on the nearby wall and pulled down the short leather strap that was hanging on it. "I made a mistake before," he said. "I was too lenient. I will not make that mistake again."

"No!" Mike struggled. "You can't beat me! I didn't do anything wrong!"

But Mr. Friedrich raised the strap and brought it down with a crack on Mike's legs.

"No!" Mike shouted again. As he bent and twisted, trying to escape, the blow was so painful that tears blurred his eyes.

"Stop!" Reuben's voice from the doorway startled both Mike and Mr. Friedrich, who straightened and turned.

"This is not your affair," Mr. Friedrich snapped.

"I am not going to let you beat Mike," Reuben said.

Mr. Friedrich's words came out in a slow hiss, "And I am not going to let a hired hand—or whoever you are—interfere with the way I raise a boy in my care."

"You do not raise a boy by beating him."

"My father raised five sons, and he could be proud of each of them. He never spared a beating when it was necessary. I should have remembered this, before it was too late."

"How could a beating ever be necessary? It is simply a large, strong man causing pain to a boy too small to fight back."

"You are wrong. As my father said, a beating is one sure way of teaching a child to behave properly. And any boy of mine—" Suddenly Mr. Friedrich stopped speaking.

Reuben was insistent. "You'll only teach this boy that some day he can be large and strong enough to hurt someone else who is defenseless."

"You have no right to say these things!" Mr. Friedrich's voice rose, and the red rims around his eyes widened. "You say you live as a laborer. You drift from job to job, never amounting to anything. I am a hardworking, prosperous citizen who has earned his position."

Reuben shook his head sadly. *"Those who have wealth must be watchful and wary. Power, alas! naught but misery brings!"*

"What do you mean?" Mr. Friedrich demanded. "Are you threatening me?"

"I was simply quoting Thomas Haynes Bayly."

"Who is Bayly? Is he the one who has sent you here? What does he want from me?"

"Sent me here?" Reuben looked puzzled. "Bayly is long dead, but when he was alive he was a poet, a man of great observations."

"Ach! Poet!" Mr. Friedrich spat his contempt.

Reuben took a few steps forward, holding out a hand. "If there was a lesson to be learned, Michael has already learned it. Come now, Mr. Friedrich. You are hungry, and your supper will be cold."

"For your information, I am always watchful," Mr. Friedrich muttered. His eyes narrowed, and he peered at Reuben with suspicion, then dropped his hand from Mike's shoulder.

Mike quickly stumbled off, trying to knead away the pain that throbbed from the spot where he'd been gripped so tightly.

"Hang up the strap. You won't need it again," Reuben told him.

Mr. Friedrich glanced at the strap, then at Mike, as though he didn't remember why Mike was there. He blinked a few times and grumbled, "Michael, you will go to bed without your supper, and there will be no more misbehavior on your part." Without another word he flung the strap to the ground and strode from the barn.

Mike took Reuben's hand and looked up at him. "Thank you," he whispered.

"I'm sorry he hurt you," Reuben said.

"I was telling the truth," Mike said. "I hope you believe me."

Reuben nodded. "I do." He picked up the lantern, leading Mike toward the house. The night air was cold and smelled of rotting leaves and rain, so they quickened their steps.

"He thinks someone sent you after him," Mike said. "He's afraid of you. Do you know why?"

"No." Reuben shrugged. "I'm just a quiet, hardworking man who is waiting to go back to the river I love. He knows that."

"He suspects that you're someone else." Mike stopped and tugged at Reuben's arm. Fear trickled down his backbone like drops of icy water. "I think I've figured out what happened! Mr. Friedrich murdered someone named Ulrich in Germany, so he ran away to the United States. All along he's been afraid someone would come after him, and now he thinks you're the one. He's killed someone before, Reuben. What if he decides to kill you, too?"

Reuben put a hand on Mike's shoulder. "You have no proof of any of this. It's all what you imagine to have happened. Haven't you ever heard the expression, 'Give a man the benefit of the doubt'?"

"Why won't you listen?"

Reuben smiled. "I've listened. I'll think about your advice, and in turn I'll give you some of my own. Those who must live with Gunter should be watchful and wary, too."

Mike saw the twinkle in Reuben's eyes, but he answered seriously. "That I'll be, never fear. Gunter will never again get the better of me."

Later, Mike climbed into bed and burrowed his face into his feather pillow to shut out the tantalizing smells of the food the others were eating. As he thought of what Gunter had done to him, anger sizzled like a burning log inside his chest. Into the darkness he vowed, "Gunter will get his due, and I'll find out what Mr. Friedrich is afraid of, no matter what."

11

"GET UP!" Mr. Friedrich shouted. "Be quick about it!" Mike groaned as the hammering on his door awoke him from sleep. He rubbed his fingers through his hair as he tried to remember exactly what he had heard during the night. There had been an argument. Loud voices—Reuben's and Mr. Friedrich's. Had they been part of his dreams, or had they been real?

Mike shook away the trailing edges of sleep and confusion. He leaned over the basin, splashing cold water on his face and rubbing it briskly with the towel.

As usual, a lantern glowed from inside the barn. On Sundays the animals had to be tended even earlier than during the week. Mike quickly dressed and slipped from the house to join Reuben. Although his stomach rumbled loudly from hunger, he'd eat later in the kitchen with Reuben rather than suffer through a miserable meal with Gunter and Mr. Friedrich. He understood now why Marta preferred to eat in the kitchen.

Reuben was pouring full buckets of milk into the large milk can when Mike entered the barn. He smiled a good morning at Mike and worked at his usual steady pace, so Mike decided that the argument he had heard was just part of his troublesome dreams and let it vanish from his mind.

After Reuben and Mike forked clean hay into the stalls, they went to the kitchen, where Marta dished up heaping plates of ham and biscuits swimming in a thick milk gravy for them. "If you want more, there is plenty," she said, and went back to work cleaning squash and stringing beans, all the while humming to herself.

The salty, creamy fragrance that rose from the plates tickled Mike's nose and made him suddenly aware of his hunger. Without pausing, he gobbled down every bite of the food and mopped up the last puddle of gravy with a warm biscuit.

When Mike finally dropped his fork onto his plate, Marta rested a hand on his shoulder and smiled at him. "You did not get a bath last night, so Mr. Friedrich wants you to bathe all over with the water in your basin." She winked and lowered her voice. "Don't look so horrified. I've heated some water over the fire. Take the kettle with you and—here—this extra towel. The others are busy dressing for their trip to the church. They won't see you with the kettle, if you hurry."

Mike grinned his thanks, grabbed the kettle, and raced up the stairs.

He seemed to be always racing, always running, always being jarred from sleep, and he wished for just one quiet, peaceful moment.

He stripped off his clothes and scrubbed all over. The room was chilly, but the hot water and soap felt good. Mike dressed in trousers, shirt, and a jacket that Gunter had long ago outgrown. The trousers were much too full, so he pulled them in tightly with the piece of rope he used for a belt. The shirt had been washed so often that the material was thin, and the sleeves of the jacket were too long, but Mike didn't mind. The shirt was soft, and he could tuck his hands inside the long sleeves to keep them warm. He pulled on his socks, boots, outer coat, cap, and gloves and clomped down the stairs, with the empty kettle hidden under the towel until he was safely in the kitchen. ✓

"Hurry, hurry! Be off with you!" Marta opened the door and shooed him from the kitchen with a gentle push. "The Friedrichs are all in the wagon, ready for their ride to church. If you were any later, they wouldn't wait for you!"

The wagon was already under way. Mike hesitated. It wasn't his fault if they wouldn't wait, was it? Then he could sit by the kitchen fire and talk with Marta and Reuben and maybe hear more river stories and even some poetry. And it wouldn't surprise him a bit if . . .

"Do you want to be in even more trouble than you are now?" Marta hissed.

"No!" Mike answered. He raced toward the wagon and managed to scramble up the back, then flopped into the empty wagon bed as the wheels jounced and shuddered through the ruts on the drive. As the horses made a sharp turn to pull the wagon onto the road, Mike struggled for balance but was tossed onto his back. He squirmed into a fairly comfortable position and lay back contentedly with his head on the palms of his hands, looking up at the threads of gray and white clouds that scudded over a pale sky. Reuben had said there was a difference in the sky over land and the sky over water. There was so much that Reuben had seen that Mike would like to see, too.

"Sit up properly," Mr. Friedrich's voice boomed.

Obediently Mike did, clinging to the side of the hard wagon bed. He wished there were a folded quilt in the wagon to cushion the hard jolts on his backside, but there was nothing besides a large hamper of food, a large folded piece of canvas, and himself. He tucked the canvas underneath his bottom, but it was every bit as firm and uncomfortable as the wagon bed.

"Marta is a stubborn girl," Mr. Friedrich said to his wife. "I think she refuses to go with us to church just to show she is angry with me for not allowing Corey Blair to see her."

Mike held his breath, listening intently.

"Do not think hard of her," Mrs. Friedrich said. "Marta is more comfortable in her own church than she is in ours."

"She should respect my wishes," Mr. Friedrich said. "That is all she needs to concern herself with." He paused for a moment, then added, "I am worried that she will not be as loyal to us as she should be."

"I—I have talked to her." Mrs. Friedrich's voice rose as she nervously clutched at her husband's arm. "We must trust her. There is nothing else we can do."

Mr. Friedrich turned to give his wife a long, hard stare before he said, "Oh yes, there is something else."

"Hans! What do you mean?"

"Never mind," he said. "This is not the time to talk about it. We will talk of something else."

He began to discuss a new cream separator he had heard of, and Mike leaned back against the side of the wagon and tried to concentrate.

Was Marta in danger, too? If Mr. Friedrich couldn't trust her, what was it he had in mind to do? Mike shuddered. He wished Marta would stay away from Corey, but he knew she wouldn't. He'd seen the way she'd bustled about the kitchen this morning. He'd heard her humming to herself. Was he the only one who guessed that Corey would ignore everything that Mr. Friedrich

99

had told him and would visit Marta while the Friedrichs were gone?

As his mind wandered he thought about himself. Sooner or later Mr. Friedrich would begin to wonder how much he knew about what they had done, and Mr. Friedrich would come up with a plan to get rid of him. Who'd miss a poor, homeless boy? No one—even Andrew MacNair—would question whatever they said about him. "How sad," the Friedrichs would sigh. "Poor Michael fell into the well and drowned." Or, "That ungrateful boy ran away. Where did he go? We have no idea." Mike shuddered, in dread fear for his life. And Reuben? Marta? How was he going to manage to save any of them?

Mike's mind was still in a turmoil when he heard other horses and voices and realized they had arrived at the church grounds. Dutifully he climbed from the wagon and followed Mr. Friedrich and Gunter at a safe distance into the church. Gunter sat on the bench to the left of his father, and Mr. Friedrich pulled Mike down on his right. On the other side of the church Mrs. Friedrich—smiling and murmuring—seated herself with the women.

Mike liked the singing. He found himself aching with longing to hear Ma's strong, full voice. Oh, if she were only here, wouldn't everyone in this building know it and be glad for it!

Mr. Friedrich nudged him sharply with an elbow, and Mike sang louder, stumbling through the unfamiliar hymn. Thankful when they had reached the last note, he flopped into his place on the bench. He tried not to daydream during the rest of the service, well aware of Mr. Friedrich's sharp elbow, but his thoughts kept skittering. The preacher spoke about loving thy neighbor, which Mike decided he agreed with. He liked the Blairs, although he couldn't understand why they believed in slavery. Mike thought he knew how it felt to be a slave. He threw a quick

100

glance sideways at Mr. Friedrich, hoping the man couldn't read his thoughts.

But it turned out not to be just neighbors like the Blairs the preacher was talking about, but everybody. *Ridiculous!* Mike thought. There was no way he wanted to love the judge who had threatened him with Tombs Prison, or Mr. Crandon, or Mr. Friedrich, or Gunter. Sure and the preacher might have a fine idea of what heaven would be like, but the man didn't know the Friedrichs very well or he'd think twice about that business of loving everyone.

When the service was over, people met outside, clustering in groups to talk and laugh. Mike noticed that although a number of the women were friendly with Mrs. Friedrich, not too many of the men came to talk to Mr. Friedrich. Two girls with pigtails down their backs stared with curiosity at Mike, but they stuck out their tongues when they saw Gunter and ran away giggling.

Some of the women had already spread cloths on the ground and were putting out bowls of food from the baskets they had brought, but Mr. Friedrich glanced impatiently at the sky, which was muddying to a darker gray, and strode over to the cluster of women around his wife. He touched the brim of his hat to them, then reached for her arm and pulled her from the group. "We will start home now. I want to get back before it begins to rain."

"But we haven't eaten," Mrs. Friedrich complained.

"We will eat in the wagon."

Mike saw Mrs. Friedrich look at her friends with longing. "I look forward to this time to talk." Her eyes lit up. "I just discovered that Evelina Pritchard and her husband will be blessed with their first little one in late spring."

"We have no time for gossip," Mr. Friedrich snapped. "I have no liking for a long ride in a downpour."

It took only a few moments for Mrs. Friedrich to say good-bye to her friends. Mike climbed back into the wagon bed, and Gunter hoisted the basket up to the front seat.

To bolster his courage as they drove down the road toward home, Mike began to hum under his breath, "Three fat sausages, Gunter in the middle ..." His stomach began to rumble so loudly he wondered if they'd think it was thunder, and he clapped a hand over his mouth to smother the laughter that welled up inside him.

Mr. Friedrich turned his head and motioned to Mike. "Here is your share. Come up here and get it."

Mike crawled to a spot just behind the wagon seat and reached up for a cloth bulging with food. He opened it on his lap and moistened his lips as he looked down at a feast of apples, molasses cake, and cold meat. Balancing himself against the dips and lurches of the wagon, he enjoyed every bite of his meal.

Although the sky grew darker, it had not begun to rain by the time the horses turned into the Friedrichs' front yard.

"We could have stayed," Mrs. Friedrich complained. "Alma had a new length of blue silk cloth, sent to her by her parents in Virginia. I wanted to hear about it and how she would style her dress."

Suddenly Mr. Friedrich pulled up the horses so sharply that they all had to fight to maintain their balance. "Hans!" Mrs. Friedrich cried. "What are you doing?"

Mike shuddered at the tone of Mr. Friedrich's voice, which was every bit as low and threatening as the sky, as he demanded, "Whose horse is that?"

Mike climbed to his knees to peer over Gunter's shoulder at the horse that was tied to the hitching post. He immediately recognized the spotted gray and gasped.

Of course—they had come home long before they had been expected.

Gunter let out an explosive giggle and said, "Papa, you know who owns that horse! It belongs to Corey Blair!"

12

REUBEN CAME FROM the house to tend to the Friedrichs' horses and wagon, the dogs at his heels. Mike followed Reuben back to the barn to lend a hand and to be far from Mr. Friedrich when his fury erupted. Even from the barn he could hear the argument as it spilled from the house into the front yard. He couldn't resist peeking from just inside the door to see what was happening.

Mr. Friedrich shook with anger. "I gave an order!" he shouted at Corey. "You disobeyed me!"

"No rule says I got to obey you!" Corey yelled back.

"This is my property!"

"But Marta ain't! We can see each other anytime she wants."

"She is a fool to waste her time with a young scalawag like you!"

Corey's voice lowered, and he leaned threateningly toward Mr. Friedrich. "You got no right to talk like that. You better be careful, Mr. Friedrich."

"Or what?" Mr. Friedrich blustered. "Or you and your ruffian brothers will come to steal and burn my property as you do with the Kansas settlers?"

Corey took another step forward and raised a fist.

Mrs. Friedrich, who had come onto the porch with Marta, gave a little shriek. "No, Corey!" Marta shouted. "Don't pay attention to what he says! Go home now! Please!"

There was silence for a moment as the two men stood like frozen statues in the yard. Then Corey untied the reins of his horse and climbed into the saddle. As the horse galloped onto the road, Mike exhaled with a whoosh, then heard a noise behind him and realized he hadn't been the only one holding his breath.

"A man with a violent temper is a dangerous man," Reuben murmured. Mike knew he wasn't talking about Corey.

At that moment Mr. Friedrich exploded in Marta's direction. "You tried to deceive me! I will not allow you to do that!"

Marta only gave a flip of her skirt and said calmly, "Very well. I will pack immediately. Reuben can drive me to St. Joe. It will not take long for me to find a family who will appreciate the hard work I do."

Mrs. Friedrich grabbed Marta around the shoulders and clung to her. "You can't leave us!" she shouted. "Hans! Think about what you are saying!"

"I am the one who gives the orders here," he grumbled.

"Hans!"

Mr. Friedrich sputtered for a few moments, then seemed to get himself under control. "Marta," he said, looking up at her, "I want you to stay."

"Very well," Marta said, "but only until I make my decision."

"What does that mean?" Mr. Friedrich demanded of Marta.

"My private thoughts are my own," she said and disappeared into the house, Mrs. Friedrich rushing after her.

Mike admired Marta's courage. Frances would have been just as brave, he thought, and for a moment he pictured his sister flouncing through the door with the same toss of her head. But Marta couldn't stay for long. She'd have to leave this house.

Marta didn't know that her life was in danger. Mike would have to find a way to talk to Marta privately and tell her what he had overheard.

Suddenly Mike found himself being pulled back into the barn. "Be quiet," Reuben whispered. "All his anger hasn't been spent. He'll be looking for someone to vent it on, and I don't want it to be you."

"Gunter!" Mike heard Mr. Friedrich yell. "Have you done your studies? Why are you wasting your time when there are things to be done?"

"But Papa!" Gunter whined, and Mike could hear the front door slam behind them.

"I have to talk to Marta," Mike whispered to Reuben. "I think she might be in danger."

"Not now," Reuben said. "Nothing is going to happen to Marta. She's well able to take care of herself."

"But—"

"Listen to me," Reuben told Mike. "Go quietly into the house through the back door and change your clothes. Try not to be noticed. We'll go into the woods, and I'll read to you. We'll have an hour or so of rest before it's time to take care of the evening chores."

Mike hesitated. "Do you really think that Marta will be safe?"

"Yes," Reuben said. "I do."

"How much do you really know about Mr. Friedrich?" Mike asked.

"No more talk about Mr. Friedrich." Reuben's voice

was firm. "If you want to go with me, then do as I say."

"Right," Mike said, and he raced toward the house.

The afternoon was a pleasant one. Reuben seemed to taste the words as he read them aloud. His voice was as soothing as water slipping over stones or wind humming through the pines. Mike didn't understand everything the poets meant to say, but even later, as he tended the animals, the words rested comfortably in his mind.

But at supper Mr. Friedrich still simmered with anger, and Mike was careful not to do anything that might cause that anger to boil over like thick soup in an undersized pot.

Mike was grateful when supper had ended and he could go to his room to get ready for bed. He opened the window only an inch, wanting the fresh air but none of the chill that too much of it would bring. Mindful that Mr. Friedrich's hammering at his door would come only too soon, Mike scrunched down under the quilt and tumbled quickly into sleep.

He knew he had not slept long when the grumble of angry voices woke him. At first he wondered if they were again part of a bad dream, but as he groggily sat up he knew it was a real argument he was hearing, and it was coming from the direction of the barn.

Moving quietly to keep the floorboards from creaking, Mike crept to the window and knelt with his arms on the sill, looking out into the night.

The barn door was open. Mr. Friedrich and Reuben stood just inside. Mr. Friedrich's long shadow waved and wobbled grotesquely in the flickering lantern light. "You woolgathering book reader!" Mr. Friedrich shouted. "You are not worth what I am paying you! I am feeding a pack of leeches who turn on me, who take advantage of my good nature."

107

Mike couldn't see Reuben or hear his answer except for the low murmur of his words. Was Reuben angry, too?

"Yes, I mean Marta, and the boy, too!" Mr. Friedrich snapped.

Again Reuben spoke, the sound of his words clipped, his answer short.

"Oh, I know all about you!" Mr. Friedrich's voice grew even louder. "I know why you're here, what you're after! Well, it won't do you any good!"

Still Mike couldn't hear what Reuben was saying, but in answer Mr. Friedrich raised a fist and shook it. "You dare to talk to me like that?" He moved farther into the barn, out of sight, but his shadow jerked violently as though it were lunging toward someone. Mike strained and heard the sound of a dull thump.

Now Mike strained with all his might, but heard nothing more. The barn was silent, and even the shadow had disappeared. Mike shivered and waited, scarcely able to breathe as he stared at the barn.

The moonlight grew stronger, and soon Mr. Friedrich appeared again. In one hand he carried the lantern. In the other he held a shovel. He began to walk toward the hill. Suddenly, as though he were aware that someone was watching, he looked up at the house. Mike ducked so quickly that he banged his forehead against the windowsill. He crouched below the window, rubbing his aching head and hoping that Mr. Friedrich hadn't seen him. He waited for the sound of the back door closing.

When the sound didn't come, he slowly, carefully, raised his head until he could see out of the window. Mr. Friedrich was not in sight. Neither was Reuben.

Mike watched at the window until his eyes grew too heavy to keep open. He felt himself dozing and forced himself to stay awake. With the barn door open and Mr. Friedrich outside somewhere, Mike knew that whatever had taken place wasn't over. He forced back the worries and fears that tried to crowd into his mind, not allowing himself to guess at what had happened.

It was painful to stay awake. His head was so heavy that his neck was sore and his eyes burned, but Mike refused to give up.

When the clang of metal woke him, Mike realized he had been sleeping in a crumpled heap on the floor. For how long? He scrambled to his knees and saw Mr. Friedrich pick up the shovel he must have dropped, then enter the barn. In a few moments he emerged, shut and barred the doors, and walked toward the house.

Mike scurried to get back into bed before Mr. Friedrich came into the kitchen. If he heard footsteps over his head, he'd know that Mike was awake. Shivering, Mike huddled under the quilt, his feet chunks of ice. What had Mr. Friedrich done? Where was Reuben? Why would Mr. Friedrich be using a shovel so late at night? Mike tugged the quilt over his head as though it would shut out all the terrifying answers.

He wished he could talk to someone. He thought of his sensible and practical sister Megan. She'd chase away all his wild, irrational fears and tell him, "You know your imagination sometimes gets the best of you, Mike. In the morning you'll work with Reuben just as you have been doing. If it will make you feel better, then tell him about the argument you overheard. He'll probably quote some line of poetry about it, and you'll know there was nothing to be afraid of."

"Megan's right," Mike murmured, so comforted that he immediately went to sleep.

In the morning Mike ate a hearty breakfast, even though Mr. Friedrich spoke to no one, and Marta slammed down the bowls of porridge so hard that cream sloshed over the edges. Gunter glowered at his food, which didn't keep him from gobbling it as though he were in a race, but Mrs. Friedrich just nibbled at her breakfast, stopping often to pat at her lips or eyes with her wrinkled napkin.

Mike could hardly wait to talk to Reuben.

He had no sooner folded his napkin beside his plate when Mr. Friedrich threw his own napkin down on the table and shoved back his chair, the legs screeching against the wooden floor. "You have learned how to milk the cows?" he asked Mike.

"Yes, sir," Mike answered, "but Reuben usually—"

"Today you and Gunter will do it," Mr. Friedrich said.

Mike stared at Gunter, who didn't look up. "But this is Monday, and Gunter has school."

"Gunter will miss school for a while. I need his help. With Reuben gone, we'll have extra work to do, so be quick about it."

"Reuben g-gone?" Mike stammered.

"That's what I said. Now hurry."

"But where—?"

Mr. Friedrich stomped from the room, and Mrs. Friedrich leaned across the table to murmur to Mike, "Hans is upset enough. Please don't ask him any questions about Reuben. It will only make him more angry."

Mike could hardly breathe. "What happened to Reuben?" he whispered.

"What happened to him? What a strange question," she answered. "He simply left us."

"Reuben wouldn't go without saying good-bye to me," Mike said.

"Well, he did." Gunter sneered. "Why should he care about saying good-bye to you, a copper-stealing guttersnipe?"

Mrs. Friedrich's hands fluttered helplessly. "Gunter, please. Boys, won't you hurry? Hans needs your help. You don't want to make him more upset than he is now, do you?"

Mike slid from his chair and went into the kitchen. He wished that Gunter would hurry outside, because he had to talk to Marta, but Gunter trailed behind Mike, slowly and methodically putting on his cap, coat, and gloves.

Mike decided to ignore him and asked Marta, "Did Reuben tell you he was going to leave?"

"No," she said, and for a moment she looked wistful. "He was not the best company at meals, with his nose always in that book of his, but he was a good, gentle man with a ready smile, and I'm sorry he has gone."

Tears burned behind Mike's eyes, and he roughly rubbed them away. "He'd tell me good-bye," he said. "I know he would."

Gunter, who had opened the back door, made a face at Mike. "You're wrong," he said, "because he didn't!"

Mr. Friedrich bellowed from the barn, "Gunter! Michael! Get out here now!"

Mike made a dash for the barn, determined to talk to Marta later. Had the argument he'd overheard been the reason for Reuben's sudden departure? Had Mr. Friedrich made him go?

Mike worked twice as hard as usual that morning because Gunter—once his father was out of sight—dawdled as much as possible and let Mike do most of the work. Mike didn't care. He ignored Gunter. He had too much to think about. He went over and over what he had seen and heard last night, and each time the picture that stood out strongly was the one of Mr. Friedrich carrying the shovel. An ugly suspicion struggled to enter Mike's thoughts, but he fought it away with hard work.

The chores went fast, in spite of Gunter's lagging. Mike was thankful when Gunter rode off with his father, who had business with a mill owner, and Mike was left to slop the pigs and hogs and clean the chicken coop.

As he washed out the feed bucket, he realized that he

had finished his chores, but Gunter and Mr. Friedrich had not returned. If he were quick about it, he'd have a few minutes of his own. There was something he had to see.

Mike ran to the cabin where Reuben had lived. The door was fastened with a padlock, but he could peer through the window. A chest, in which Reuben probably had kept his clothing, stood open, and Mike could see that it was empty. The bed was stripped, with only a bare straw mattress lying on the rope slings that held it. There was another room, beyond a partition, and Mike also inspected it through its window. It, too, was completely bare and spotlessly clean. Both rooms looked as though they had never been lived in.

So Reuben had gone, taking his few possessions with him. Mike slid to the ground, resting his head and arms on his knees. He had gone without saying good-bye.

But what had Mr. Friedrich been doing with the shovel?

Mike heard the horses and quickly scrambled to his feet. He ran away from the cabin as fast as he could and went to meet Mr. Friedrich, who had dismounted. Mike took the reins from him and led the horse into the barn, where he removed the saddle and bridle and rubbed the animal down.

From the corner of his eye, Mike saw Gunter make a few quick passes at the sweat on the neck of the horse he had been riding, then lead the animal toward one of the stalls. Mike straightened and said, "The poor horse needs more care than what you've given him."

"Do it yourself," Gunter said. He dropped the horse's reins and ran from the barn.

"Hey!" Mike grabbed for the reins before the horse took it into his head to bolt and fastened them securely. He had his hands full with both animals to care for, but he didn't mind. The work was routine and gave him time to think.

His mind recreated the scene from last night. Mr. Friedrich had raised his fist and lunged toward Reuben. But what had happened then? Mike had seen many a fight on the streets of New York City, and they were rowdy, noisy affairs, with huffing and panting and grunts, as fists smacked loudly into jaws and bodies went flying, only to scramble up and clash again. No, there had not been a fight in the barn.

What about the shovel?

A man could be struck down and killed with the blade of a shovel.

Mike gasped and leaned for a moment against one of the stalls to support his wobbling legs. He'd tried to warn Reuben. Mr. Friedrich had killed a man before. Who was to say he wouldn't kill again?

Mike studied the barn. He wasn't sure what he was searching for, but everything looked as it normally did. There were no signs of a struggle and—he gulped—no signs of blood. He put the horses into their stalls and climbed the ladder. He didn't know what he expected to find in the hayloft besides a broader view of the barn.

He lay on his stomach at the edge of the loft and stared down at the rumps of the horses and what he could see of the cleanly swept stalls for the cows. The tack was neatly in order, and the tools were stored where they belonged.

His eyes passed over the scene, and at first the small, dark red spot that protruded from behind the tool chest at the far end of the barn didn't seem important. But something made him look back. That tiny, dull red lump reminded him of something. Mike slid and scrambled down the ladder and ran to the end of the barn. His heart banged and thumped loudly enough for anyone to hear. As he reached behind the tool chest, his fingertips felt the familiar outlines of a book, and he tugged at it, pulling it out from where it was wedged.

Mike held the book in his hands and slowly opened the cover. There, at the top of the first page, was written in a firm hand, *Property of Reuben Starkey.*

Mike groaned aloud, positive now that his suspicions were correct. Reuben wouldn't have left without his book of poems. It was a possession that meant everything to him.

Mike knew now there was only one explanation. Mr. Friedrich had murdered Reuben!

Frantically Mike shoved the book into the pocket of his coat. Mr. Friedrich must never know what he had uncovered.

13

STUMBLING AND GASPING for breath, Mike ran in the direction Mr. Friedrich had taken the night before. When he reached the woods he flung himself facedown on the ground and lay without moving until his breathing had slowed and the pain was gone from his chest. He managed to climb to his feet, but his knees shook as he slowly walked into the woods, carefully searching the ground, praying he wouldn't find what he was looking for.

He parted a stand of small hickory trees and stepped through, discovering at his feet a tangle of twigs and brush that had been spread over the ground. He knelt to brush them aside and found a rectangle of tamped-down earth that recently had been spaded. Mike crumpled to the ground in despair and cried for his friend Reuben until all tears were gone and his body shuddered with dry sobs.

Finally he sat up, rubbing the tears and dirt from his

face with the sleeves of his jacket. What should he do? Who could help him?

Ma? She was too far away to help. Frances? She had told him, "If ever you need me, I'll come." But there was no quick way he could reach Frances. Now that this had happened, would Mr. Friedrich ever let him try to reach his family again? "Nobody can help me," he whispered.

As Mike tried to fight his feelings of hopelessness, Megan's voice came into his mind as clearly as though she were near him. "You have no proof, Mike. You don't know enough about what happened. It's not fair to Mr. Friedrich to jump to conclusions."

Mike nodded. That was true. He must ask careful questions. He must wait and watch. At the first clang of the bell that signaled the noon meal, Mike shivered. How could he return to the house to face Mr. Friedrich? It was easy to imagine how angry Mr. Friedrich would be if Mike were late, so he dusted himself off and raced back.

Mr. Friedrich was still in a terrible mood. He gulped great bites of food, muttering between mouthfuls about the problem of trying to find an extra farmhand. "With winter approaching not many men will be out looking for jobs," he complained.

"You will find someone." Mrs. Friedrich was obviously trying to calm him. "Maybe when we go to St. Joe for supplies."

"Until then, Papa, Mike can do Reuben's jobs." Gunter spoke between mouthfuls. "Reuben trained Mike, didn't he? Mike should earn his keep."

Mike found the courage to ask, "Why did Reuben leave?"

Mr. Friedrich scowled at Mike and replied, "Because he was an ungrateful, deceitful wretch!"

Mike choked back angry words and tried to remain calm. "Where did Reuben go?" he asked.

"How should we know?" Mr. Friedrich shouted.

"No more talk of Reuben," Mrs. Friedrich begged. "Let's be silent and finish our meal."

Mike tried to eat, but he couldn't. This time not even Mrs. Friedrich seemed to notice. He was thankful when Mr. Friedrich heaved himself to his feet and they all could leave the table.

As usual, Gunter followed his father to avoid helping. Before Mrs. Friedrich could leave the room, however, Mike touched her arm. He glanced toward the door to make sure that Mr. Friedrich was not within earshot and whispered, "Please tell me what you know about Reuben."

"He is gone. That's all I know," Mrs. Friedrich murmured. "Do not talk about him again."

"But I need to know what—what happened to him," Mike stammered. In a rush the words came out. "We were chums. I know he wouldn't have left without saying good-bye to me."

Mrs. Friedrich, her eyes also on the door, took Mike's hand and bent to whisper to him. "Reuben was rude to Mr. Friedrich. He spoke back to him. He lied to him. Without a word of apology, he packed his belongings and left. His behavior shocked all of us."

"Reuben wouldn't lie, and I can't believe that he'd be rude."

"Hans told me this himself," Mrs. Friedrich said.

"Reuben wasn't the kind who would walk away in the middle of the night without a good-bye to anyone," Mike said.

"People are not always who or what they seem," she said so quietly that Mike was sure she was hiding something.

"I know that Reuben wouldn't have left like that," Mike said. "He would have waited to say good-bye to me."

Mrs. Friedrich touched his arm with her fingertips, and for a moment her face softened. "I'm sorry, Michael," she said. "Now, please do not ask any more questions. You will only be causing trouble."

Mike gulped against the tightness in his throat and picked up a platter to carry to the kitchen. Whether Mrs. Friedrich was trying to deceive him or thought she was telling the truth, Mike didn't know. She might have been repeating the explanation her husband had given her. But it didn't explain Reuben's book of poems wedged behind the tool chest, and it didn't explain the newly turned earth hidden in the woods.

He had no chance to talk to Marta until that evening after supper. "Come outside with me," he whispered.

She nodded, grabbed her shawl, and hurried out the back door. When they had reached a safe distance from the house, Mike stopped, and Marta held out a hand, an eager smile on her face.

"You have a note from Corey?"

"No," Mike said. "I haven't seen him since he was here yesterday."

Marta's shoulders slumped. "Then why did you bring me out here in the cold?"

"To ask you about Reuben," he said.

"What would I know about Reuben?"

"The room he slept in is bare. Did you clean it? Did you see anything he might have left behind?"

"That's a strange question."

"But it's something I need to know. Did you look in the cupboard? Were any of his clothes there?"

Marta gave an impatient sigh and answered, "I cleaned his room and gathered the quilts and linens from his bed to wash them, and yes, I dusted out the cupboard. Believe me, if Reuben had left any of his possessions, I would have found them."

"Didn't he say good-bye to you?"

"No," she said. A small wrinkle appeared between her eyebrows. "I wish that he had, because I would have thanked him for holding his tongue about Corey coming to call." Suddenly her eyes became soft with sympathy, and she reached for Mike's hand. "Oh," she said, "you are hurt because he didn't tell you he was going."

"How do you know he left?" Mike asked.

"How? Because Mrs. Friedrich told me he had gone. What do you mean?"

"Did you see or hear him leave?"

She shrugged. "No, but that's because I'm a sound sleeper."

"Don't you think it's strange that he left in the middle of the night?"

Marta began to look uncomfortable and shifted from one foot to the other. "I think you should know the truth," she said, "but don't let on that I told you. Reuben didn't leave because he wanted to go. Mrs. Friedrich admitted to me that Mr. Friedrich was so angry with Reuben that he sent him away."

"Would Reuben have left without his book of poems?" Mike asked.

At this Marta smiled. "Of course not. I sometimes thought that book was attached to the man's left hand."

Mike hesitated. He didn't know how much to tell Marta. If he showed her the book and told her about the newly dug spot in the woods, what would she do? He had to know how she would react before he could explain. "I'm afraid for you," he said.

Her eyes widened. "What do you mean by that?"

Mike clutched her arm and pulled her down so that he could whisper in her ear. "On the way to church, Mr. and Mrs. Friedrich were talking about you. I don't understand all that they said, but they were worried about your loyalty to them."

Marta straightened with a snap, nearly knocking Mike off his feet. "Oh, they were, were they!"

"I'm telling you because Mrs. Friedrich said she had

talked to you, and that's all that could be done, but Mr. Friedrich said no, there was something else he could do."

"I'm sure he thinks there is," she said, her words so angry they sparked like hot coals.

"Marta," Mike asked, "does this have something to do with Ulrich?"

"Yes!" she said. "It certainly does!"

"Did you know Ulrich? Were you there when—?"

Marta's face was flushed with anger as she snapped, "Did I know Ulrich?" Her laugh was so brittle and hard that Mike shuddered. "Unfortunately," she answered, "I was Ulrich's wife!"

Before Mike could close his gaping mouth, Marta had run ahead of him into the house.

All week, Mike felt as though he were living inside of a nightmare. Marta refused to answer his questions, hushing him and sending him away, and bits of urgent, whispered conversations shivered through the house like lost ghosts. Slowly Mr. Friedrich's anger seeped away, but he was often deep in thought. *What is he seeing inside his mind?* Mike wondered, remembering the angry words and the shovel.

As Mr. Friedrich's anger abated, Mrs. Friedrich began to relax. "Michael, Michael, why do you not eat?" she asked at nearly every meal. "I thought you liked the dishes I made."

"I do," Mike answered. He made a valiant effort to clean his plate, but he swallowed each bite with difficulty.

At night he lay awake, sorting over the little he had learned. At times he convinced himself that Reuben had simply packed his things and left, as Mr. Friedrich had ordered him to do; but at other times deep shadows slithered through his thoughts, and he shivered with fear, knowing for a certainty that Reuben's body lay buried in the woods. Sometimes in his dreams he saw Reuben's face so clearly that he tried to reach out to him, but the face always disappeared, and Mike awoke, whimpering with fear.

Early Friday morning, Mike was more exhausted than usual. As he rested his head against the warm flanks of the cow he was milking, he wondered how he would last through the day. Then Mr. Friedrich announced, "We have begun our chores early, because we are going to St. Joseph today."

To St. Joseph! Mike jumped with such eagerness that the cow turned to stare at him and switched her tail in his direction. Katherine Banks was in St. Joe! He would find a chance to tell Mrs. Banks all that had happened. He knew she'd listen to what he had to say. "Will I go, too?" Mike asked, barely able to breathe until he heard the answer.

Mr. Friedrich studied him for a moment before he said, "If your work is finished in time, you may go."

"Could I mail my letters there?"

"I have already told you that I would mail them for you."

Having heard the touch of impatience in Mr. Friedrich's voice, Mike said no more. He kept a sharp watch on Gunter, afraid that Gunter might have planned something to keep him from going to St. Joe. Every now and then Mike found Gunter sneaking quick looks at him, a nasty smile flickering on his lips.

But after a hearty breakfast the family piled into the wagon, Mike again alone in the wagon bed with only Reuben's book of poems in his pocket for company.

"Doesn't Marta want to go with us?" he asked.

"Marta has her duties here," Mrs. Friedrich answered.

Would Marta see Corey again? Mike wondered. Would she decide to leave the Friedrichs? It would be terrible to lose another friend. Then no one would take his side.

He'd miss Marta, but he also hoped for her sake that she'd go.

Mike was so eager to get to St. Joe that the ride seemed to take twice as long as it should. But soon he could see clusters of houses, and the taller buildings rose above the treetops. He clung to the edge of the wagon, watching the people in other wagons, the horseback riders, and the foot traffic in the streets as they rode into town, and he jumped to his feet when Mr. Friedrich pulled his team to a halt in front of Banks General Store. Mike saw Mr. Amos Crandon just entering the store and shivered. No! Forget Mr. Crandon. This was Mrs. Banks's store, and Mike could hardly wait to greet her!

Katherine Banks saw Mike at the same time he found her, and she hurried from around the counter to sweep him up in a warm hug.

She stooped and held his face in her hands. "How are you, Mike? Is everything going well for you?"

Mike couldn't answer. He just dove into her, tightly wrapping his arms around her waist.

She ruffled his hair. "I have something for you, Mike—a letter from Frances Mary."

"Grand!" he said, then gasped at the twinkle in Katherine's eyes. "You know?" he asked.

"Her secret was discovered. She's happily back to being a girl," she said. "Come with me. I'll give you her letter, and let her explain."

"I have something to tell you," he said as she handed him the letter. "Something private."

A customer called to her, "I can't find the bolt of cotton sateen."

Before she hurried to help, Katherine said to Mike, "We'll make some private time. Just give me a few minutes."

Mike found a quiet place on the floor between the

122

tables piled with bolts of cloth and hats and furs and read his letter from Frances over and over again. He gobbled her words as though he were starving and they were food. Oh, how desperately he missed his brothers and sisters!

Mike finally realized that someone was standing over him and looked up to see Gunter. "Go away," Mike told him.

"Papa wants you," Gunter said. "Better hurry, or he'll be angry."

With a sigh Mike tucked the letter into his coat pocket and scrambled to his feet. He tried to go down the narrow aisle, but Gunter squeezed into him, roughly shoving him backward.

"What's the matter with you?" Mike demanded.

Gunter turned and said, "Papa's at the counter," then backed off and ran ahead of Mike toward his father.

As Mike joined them, Gunter tugged at his father's sleeve. "Papa!" he pointed at Mike. "I saw him steal a knife! A fine, large pocketknife!"

Everyone in the store stopped and stared at Mike.

"I didn't steal a knife!" Mike insisted. "I didn't steal anything!"

"Look in his pocket! His left coat pocket!" Gunter shouted.

Mr. Friedrich, his face dark with anger, grabbed Mike's arm in one hand and dove into his pocket with the other. He pulled out a slender pocketknife, its blade encased in a sheath of steel.

Mr. Crandon stepped forward, his eyes gleaming with triumph. "Didn't I say so?" he asked the people around him. "Once a thief, always a thief! The boy has proved me right."

Sick with misery, Mike realized that Gunter had figured out how Mike had switched Mr. Friedrich's gold watch and had tried the switch himself with the knife. *I should have thought about it when he shoved into me!* he thought. *I should have kept my wits about me and suspected what he'd do!* Mike looked from face to face, crying out, "Gunter put that knife into my pocket!"

"Lies! More lies!" Mr. Friedrich thundered.

Mr. Crandon nodded. "Michael Kelly's a thief and a liar."

"I have a pocketknife of my own. I wouldn't take another," Mike shouted.

"Be quiet!" Mr. Friedrich ordered. "We want to hear nothing more from you. A pickpocket once and always! I should not have tried to reclaim you! You belong back in New York and in prison!"

As Mr. Friedrich began to drag Mike through the store toward the wagon, Katherine Banks cried out, "Wait! Let Mike explain!"

But Mr. Friedrich shouted at Mike, "What else have you stolen? What else might be in your pockets?"

Mike twisted around, trying to break Mr. Friedrich's painful grip, and shouted at him, "Reuben Starkey's book is in my pocket! The book you tried to hide after you killed him!"

14

MR. FRIEDRICH'S EYES bulged like the eyes of a pond frog, and his mouth fell open. Only a gurgling, gasping sound came out.

Mrs. Friedrich yelped and plopped down on a nearby bale of unbleached cotton cloth.

Pushing her way from around the counter, Katherine Banks pried Mr. Friedrich's fingers from Mike's arm. At the same time, a tall man stooped to poke his face into Mr. Friedrich's, demanding, "What's this about a murder?"

"Who's Reuben Starkey?" someone asked.

"The Friedrichs' hired man," someone else explained.

"He's that book-reading river man," the tall man added.

Everyone began to talk at once. "When did this happen? Did the boy see it? Someone should get the marshal!"

"The marshal's out of town," Mr. Crandon said. He hooked his thumbs into his vest pockets and began to bluster. "Why are we listening to this boy—a known liar and thief?"

The color began to come back to Mr. Friedrich's face. "That's right!" he shouted. "We do not need the marshal! The story is nothing but lies! I did not kill Reuben! I have never killed anybody!"

"Be quiet, please!" Katherine shouted over the babble of voices. "Mike wouldn't make this accusation without a good reason. I'd like to hear what he has to say."

Mike was so frightened he could hardly talk. He had to clear his throat and try again before he could blurt out what he had seen and heard the night Reuben had disappeared.

"A stupid boy, waking from dreams. He has mixed them with reality," Mr. Friedrich grumbled. "He told you that he fell asleep again on the floor. That's why he didn't see Reuben leave the barn or see him pack his belongings and leave my property."

Mike tugged Reuben's book from his pocket and held it high, where everyone could see it. "This book of poems belongs to Reuben. He was never without it. Reuben would never have left his book behind!" He faced Mr. Friedrich as he added, "I found it where you hid it behind the tool box in the barn!"

"Reuben gave me that book!" Mr. Friedrich shouted.

"I don't believe it!" Mike shouted back.

"It was for *you*, you *Dummkopf*! He asked me to give it to you!"

Mike stared at him for an instant and hugged the book to his chest. "Then why didn't you?" he asked.

"Because you have no need to fill your mind with that foolishness. *I* will decide what you will read and learn."

He reached out for Mike, but Mike backed away, saying, "I found a newly spaded place in the woods, with brush laid over it to hide it. It's big enough, big enough for—"

Mrs. Friedrich gave a little shriek, and the tall man

clapped a hand on Mr. Friedrich's shoulder. "Big enough to bury a man?" he asked Mike.

"I think so," Mike nodded.

Mr. Friedrich sputtered, "Let go of me, Ned Gosnell! Michael doesn't know what he is talking about! Yes, I buried something, but it was not Reuben! It was—what it was is no one's business!"

"I think you had better tell us, Mr. Friedrich," Katherine said.

He studied the faces turned to his and flushed red with anger. "Very well. It was my own property, my money and my valuables which I hid from—from Corey Blair!" Mr. Friedrich quickly looked down at the floor, and Mike knew he was lying.

"Corey Blair?" a short, stocky man asked. "This is a mighty strange tale. I know the Blairs well, and their boys may be a little headstrong, but they're all good, law-abiding citizens. Corey Blair wouldn't steal Friedrich's money."

"Maybe some of us should go take a look at that dug-up place in Friedrich's woods," Ned said. "How about you, Tom?"

The stocky man nodded. "I'll come."

"And you, Amos?"

Mr. Crandon took a step backward. "I—uh—have pressing business to attend to."

"You—you—none of you have the right!" Mr. Friedrich stammered.

Katherine took Mike's hand. "I think it will be better if Mike, for the time being, stays with me."

"No!" Mr. Friedrich said. "Andrew MacNair has put me in charge of Michael's welfare, and there he will remain until I decide otherwise!"

"I disagree!" Katherine said.

Mr. Friedrich grabbed Mike's left hand and whirled,

pulling him from the group. Quickly Mike stretched out his right hand and shoved the book at Katherine.

"I'll keep it for you," she said quietly. "And I'll send for Andrew."

Mike was shoved into the bed of the wagon as Gunter leapt to the wagon seat. Mrs. Friedrich was half-lifted to the seat where she slumped, fanning herself vigorously. Ned and Tom rode their horses next to the wagon. Mike was glad they were along.

Mike's thoughts were as scrambled as broken eggs. He didn't know what to believe. Could Reuben really have left him the book of poems because he didn't have a chance to say good-bye? Or had Mr. Friedrich made up the story to save his own skin? And the closer they came to that spot in the woods, the closer they came to knowing what Mr. Friedrich had buried there.

When they arrived at the farm, Ned and Tom tied their horses to a post. Gunter was told to care for the Friedrich horses. Two shovels were brought from the barn, and Mike was marched up the hill with the men, Mr. Friedrich's large fingers digging mercilessly into his left shoulder.

They paused at the site Mike had described under the hickory trees. Carefully Ned pulled aside the brush to reveal the patch of tamped earth. "There it is," he said. "Nothin' left but to see what's buried there."

Mr. Friedrich slapped the handle of one shovel into Mike's trembling hands and gave him a push that nearly knocked him off balance. "You are responsible for this," he snarled. "You can be the one to dig."

Tom gave Mr. Friedrich a disgusted look and took the other shovel into his own hands. The loose earth flew aside in huge clumps as he worked next to Mike, and before long the metal edge of Tom's shovel thumped as it hit something hard.

Mike held his breath as dirt was scraped away to reveal a wooden box a little more than a foot square in size, its corners trimmed with brass, its hinged lid fastened tightly with a padlock.

"Couldn't fit a man into a box that small," Ned said.

"Of course you couldn't!" Friedrich snapped. "I told you what is in the box! My valuables!"

"Better take a look, just to make sure," Tom said.

Mr. Friedrich's chest puffed out. "You can take my word for it," he demanded.

"The marshal's gonna ask what we seen," Ned told him. He pointed at the padlock. "Have you got a key for that with you?"

"I—I lost the key."

Ned bent and hefted the padlock. "It's not a very strong lock. I can break it open with the shovel."

Mr. Friedrich stepped forward. "Wait. I will open it." He pulled a key from his vest pocket, stooped, and opened the lock. Hesitantly he opened the hinged lid of the box.

Mike leaned forward with the rest of them to peer inside the box. It was half-filled with coins, many of them silver, some of them gold.

"Whoo-eee!" Tom said. "That's a powerful lot of money."

Ned's eyes were sharper. "But it's not U.S. money." He looked up at Mr. Friedrich. "Where'd this come from?"

"The German states," Mr. Friedrich said. "The guldens and ducats from Prussia, the larger coins from Würzburg." He suddenly slammed the lid down and locked the box again. "I brought this with me to the United States. I have taken good care of it, and now—because of your meddling—it is no longer safe."

"We aren't going to take your money," Tom said indignantly.

"But you will tell everyone!" Mr. Friedrich spat out

the words. "The moment you are back to town your tongues will wag faster than a dog's tail!"

"I won't give that remark the answer it deserves," Tom said, and Mike could see him swallow hard, "because we *are* on your property, but you got no call to insult us like that."

When Mr. Friedrich didn't answer, the two men looked at each other. "Want us to bury it here again?" Ned asked.

"No! Do you think I am stupid?" Mr. Friedrich screeched.

The two men hoisted the box to ground level, and Mr. Friedrich struggled to pick it up. "Are you satisfied now that this boy has been lying?" he demanded as he cradled the box in his arms.

Both men turned to study Mike.

"I thought—" Mike began. "I thought that—" He took a long breath. "When Reuben disappeared in the middle of the night after that argument with Mr. Friedrich, I was afraid. I'm—I'm sorry I told everyone what I thought had happened."

Ned shot an angry glance toward Mr. Friedrich and clapped a hand on Mike's shoulder. "No real harm done," he said. "Matter of fact, we still don't know what happened to that Starkey feller, do we?"

"I told you that Reuben Starkey left!" Mr. Friedrich exploded. "You are all such idiots to believe that boy! Get off my property! Right now!"

"Now just hold on a minute," Tom said.

"I don't know how we'll reach an answer to this unless someone can find Starkey," Ned said. "If you don't know where—"

Mr. Friedrich interrupted. "Go back to town and report what you found to those other stupid fools!" He glared at the men. "And tell them there is no use their looking for my money, because by the time they come

130

sneaking around my land, I will have these things hidden somewhere else!"

Tom's chin jutted out, and he muttered, "You're accusin' a lot of good folks of being fools and thieves!"

He stepped toward Mr. Friedrich, but Ned put a restraining hand on his arm. "Tom, we'll give folks the message just like Friedrich gave it to us. And we'll tell the marshal there wasn't no sign of Reuben Starkey. Maybe he'll want to come out and do some more digging around this property."

"Go!" Mr. Friedrich shouted. "Get out of here!"

The men strode down the hill. Mr. Friedrich waited until they were out of sight, then snapped at Mike, "Come to the house, and bring those shovels with you."

Mike struggled with the two shovels, trying to keep up with Mr. Friedrich, who strode quickly in spite of the heavy box he carried. As they reached the house, Mr. Friedrich ordered, "Wait right here," then went inside.

Trembling, Mike clung to the shovels until Mr. Friedrich reappeared.

"To the barn," Mr. Friedrich ordered.

Inside the barn Mr. Friedrich grabbed the shovels and threw them against the wall. "Mrs. Banks will send for Andrew MacNair," he said, "and I will tell him what a troublemaker you have been. But I will tell him that I have decided *not* to send you back to New York. It is my duty to teach you to conquer your wicked nature and learn to be a responsible man. Mr. MacNair will agree with me. No one else will take you, and MacNair will not want to send you back to New York. I want you to think about what this means and about the gratitude you owe me, so until tomorrow morning you will be locked in your room upstairs."

"Mr. Friedrich," Mike tried to say, "I know I was wrong to accuse you without knowing the facts about Reuben, but I was frightened, and you wouldn't believe that I hadn't taken that pocketknife, that Gunter had slipped it into my pocket."

"You are a wicked boy." Mr. Friedrich's low tone of voice frightened Mike more than when he had been shouting at him. Mike's stomach clutched painfully. Mr. Friedrich continued, "Do you know that people will come and trample my land, looking for a grave that does not exist? And even though they find nothing, forever after there will be those who will still believe that I killed Reuben Starkey."

"If we could find Reuben—if we knew where to search for him, then people would—"

"Before you are locked up," Mr. Friedrich said, as though Mike's words were no more than the buzzing of a fly, "you will be given the punishment you deserve."

As Mike realized what Mr. Friedrich meant, he tried to run, but Mr. Friedrich was faster. With his left hand he gripped Mike's arm, and he managed to tug off Mike's coat. Flinging it on the ground, he pulled the strap from the wall. As Mike twisted and squirmed, Mr. Friedrich brought down the strap across his legs and shoulders, crying out, "Ulrich! You are Ulrich all over again!"

Finally he dropped the strap and let go of Mike, who fell to the ground, racked by burning pain. He closed his eyes to shut it out, but stabbing streaks of white-hot light flashed through the darkness.

"Get up," Mr. Friedrich ordered. When Mike didn't move, Mr. Friedrich reached down and jerked him to his feet. Mike could hardly walk, but Mr. Friedrich poked and prodded him into the house and through the kitchen, where Marta stared at him with damp, red-rimmed eyes.

Upstairs, Mr. Friedrich shoved Mike roughly into his room. Mike threw himself facedown on the bed. As he heard the key turn in the lock and footsteps thump down the stairs, he burst into tears. However horrible prison might be, this life had to be worse. "I never meant to cause so much trouble, Ma," he murmured through his sobs.

Gradually it seemed to Mike as though his family had gathered to be with him in the room. Each of them looked at him with such a deep sadness it broke his heart. Ma held out her arms to him, and he struggled to reach her, but she stood too far away. There were tears on Peg's cheeks, and Frances softly called his name, but Mike hurt so much he couldn't leave the bed.

"What should I do?" he whispered.

Danny's eyes flashed. "Run away! Head for the mountains," he insisted.

Megan shook her head firmly. "That won't solve anything." She brushed back her dark hair and said, "Think, Mike. Think hard."

"Think about what?" little Petey asked.

"Mike knows." Frances held out a hand to Mike and smiled. "Where would Reuben go?"

Mike groaned. "I don't know."

"Yes, you do!"

"Let him rest." Da moved forward as he spoke and began to stroke back the damp hair from Mike's forehead.

"It's your fault, Da!" Mike accused. "This happened because you left us!"

"Do you think I wanted to? I would never have left you willingly, Mike, my lad." There was so much pain in Da's voice that Mike pulled himself up and grasped his hand with all the strength he could find.

"I wanted to help," Mike explained. "Sometimes I was so fearful, and I didn't know what to do. I tried. I—"

"Hush, son. It's all right." Da put a finger over Mike's lips and whispered, "I love you, Mike."

"Oh, Da!" As he looked deeply into his father's eyes, the wall of anger and pain around him shattered, and Mike clung tightly to Da. "I need you," he murmured.

"I'm here," Da answered. "I'm here." His words blended

133

with the gentle stroking of his hand to ease the pain, and soon Mike was breathing with the soft, steady rhythm. "I'm here. I'm here."

Frances stood beside Da. "You've never been down for long, Mike. You've got spunk and wit, and you know what to do next."

She held out a hand and opened her mouth to speak again, but a voice intruded. Mike's dream vanished as Marta whispered, "Mike! Mike, wake up!"

He raised his head, rubbing sleep from his eyes, and managed slowly and achingly to sit up.

"Your poor, poor back," she murmured. "There's blood on your shirt. Mr. Friedrich has no right to take out his anger on you." From under Mike's coat, which she laid on the chair, she pulled out a thick parcel and shoved it into his hands. "There's meat and bread in there," she whispered. "Hide the paper when you're finished."

"Where's Mr. Friedrich?"

"He and Gunter are at work outside, and Mrs. Friedrich has taken to her bed."

"How did you get into my room? The door was locked."

Marta sat beside him on the bed. "Mr. Friedrich hung the key in its place in the kitchen. I just waited until I knew he would not be back for a while."

"I don't want to get you into trouble."

"It doesn't matter to me one whit how much he might shout at me." She lifted her chin. "I have made my decision. I am going to leave this place."

"To marry Corey?"

"Maybe," she said. "But first I will find work elsewhere. It won't be hard."

"Last night, while he was beating me, Mr. Friedrich called me Ulrich," Mike said. "Do you know why?"

She nodded, her cheeks flushing pink. "Because Ulrich was a thief. Mr. Friedrich has never been able to forgive

134

him for that. You see, Ulrich was his son—his eldest son."

Mike gasped. "You told me you were married to Ulrich."

"I was very young, and my parents had just died," Marta said. "There was much poverty where we lived, but at least the Friedrichs had food on the table, and Ulrich was handsome and funny and ..." She paused. "The Friedrichs had food because of Ulrich."

Mike felt his own face become hot with embarrassment. "What happened to Ulrich?"

"He was finally caught and taken to jail. Mr. Friedrich was so furious with Ulrich that he would not go to see him or help him in any way, even when Ulrich became very ill."

"Is that how Ulrich died?"

"Yes, and Mr. Friedrich blames himself."

"How about the—?"

"Hush!" Marta put a finger to her lips and glanced toward the doorway. Neither of them moved or even dared to breathe, until she said, "I thought I heard someone. We must not talk any longer."

She turned to leave, but Mike said, "Wait. I need your help." The pieces of his dream began to fall into place, and he knew what Frances and Megan had tried to tell him. *No matter what's in store for me,* he thought, *Michael Patrick Kelly's never going to stay down and out for long.*

"I'm going to leave, too," he told Marta. "I have to look for Reuben. Bringing Reuben back to St. Joe is the only way I'll be able to change people's minds about Mr. Friedrich."

Her eyes widened. "You would do that for him, after what he's done to you?"

"I owe him that," Mike said.

"Then leave," Marta said. "Leave tonight, while the

135

family is asleep, so they won't know for hours that you have gone. I'll see that the door is unlocked."

Mike shook his head. "Those stairs creak loudly enough to raise the whole family from sleep. I'll have to leave through the window."

Marta frowned. "The drop could break your legs."

"Not if I had a rope," Mike said.

Marta smiled. "You'll have your rope. I can get it for you." She went to the door and paused. "Good luck, Mike. I hope we'll meet again in happier times."

The door shut, and the key made a grating click in the lock.

Mike held his breath, the food in his hands forgotten. His heart hammered in his ears. Tonight he was going to run away!

15

MIKE LET GO of the rope and dropped the last few feet to the ground. When Mr. Friedrich discovered the rope, he'd think that Mike must have hidden it in his room and planned this escape for a long time. He'd never believe *why* Mike had run away. *One more strike against you, Michael, my lad,* he thought. If only he could find Reuben and try to make things come out right!

Although Mike could find his way around New York City streets at night with no trouble at all, the heavy blackness that swallowed the open countryside made it difficult to travel. With only a thin moon to light the way—a moon often hidden by drifting clouds—Mike occasionally stumbled as he walked the long road toward St. Joseph. His knees and the palms of his hands stung from his falls, and his back and legs still throbbed with pain from the leather strap, but he wouldn't allow himself to stop. He had to reach the river landing where there'd be boatmen who might have seen Reuben. Thankfully, as his eyes grew accustomed to the darkness, he was able to pick up his pace, and even though he had lost any notion of the time, it was still before dawn when he reached the houses on the outskirts of St. Joe. As he passed the first ones, Mike began to run toward the river.

There were lights on the water and men moving about, although most of the stern-wheelers were moored. The Missouri River was treacherous enough in the daytime, Reuben had told Mike. At night it was even worse, a dark, deep ribbon of hidden logs and rocks which could rip out the bottom of a large boat.

Light spilled from some of the buildings near the landing, and from the nearest one came voices raised in loud laughter and piano music. Mike stopped under its swinging, creaking sign as he saw a group of men approaching from down the street. He went to meet them, asking, "Have any of you gents seen a man called Reuben Starkey?"

Two of the men shook their heads. "Who's he?" one muttered. But a short, wiry man said, "Haven't seen the man, but I've been hearin' things about him."

Mike let out a long sigh of relief. "Do you know where he is?" It was hard for him to keep from grabbing the man's arm in his eagerness.

The man chuckled and elbowed a companion in his ribs. "Depends on what story you want to believe. I heard tell that Starkey vanished, and word is that he was murdered in cold blood." As Mike groaned, the man said, "On the other hand, a couple'a days ago someone told me he'd just talked to Starkey."

"Who was it? Where is he?"

"Don't recollect," the man said. "I just remember he said Starkey told him he was heading upriver."

The men, impatient to be inside the saloon, edged past Mike, who hesitated, wondering where to go next.

He had turned, his back to the door, when suddenly a voice spoke so close behind him that he jumped.

"Watch where you're going, boy!"

Mike stumbled aside to let the man leave the saloon, but a hand clamped on his shoulder, and he cried out.

"What's this? The Kelly boy!"

A face leaned to peer into his own, and Mike groaned. Mr. Crandon!

"Trying to run away, are you?" Mr. Crandon demanded.

"No!" Mike insisted. "I came to try to find Reuben!"

A few men had joined them, curiosity in their eyes, and Mike looked to them pleadingly. "Has even one of you seen Reuben Starkey, who works the flatboats?" But they shook their heads. "I have to find him!" Mike cried out.

"A likely excuse for your running off in the middle of the night," Mr. Crandon said. "Well, you won't find me as lenient toward your shortcomings as the Friedrichs have been. Come with me." He gripped Mike's upper right arm and almost jerked him off his feet.

"W-Where are you taking me?" Mike stammered.

"Since neither the marshal nor MacNair's in town, I'm going to turn you over to Mrs. Banks, who can see with her own eyes how wrong she was to trust you."

Mike gasped with relief, then knew that Mr. Crandon had misinterpreted it when the man smiled smugly and gave a satisfied grunt. He pulled Mike down the street and up a nearby hill. Mike had to run to keep up with Mr. Crandon's long steps, but he went with the man willingly. Katherine Banks would understand. If anyone could help him, she'd be the one.

They reached the top of the hill before Mr. Crandon stopped, puffing and coughing and wheezing for breath, in front of a short flight of steps that led to a trim clapboard house facing the river. Not releasing his grip on Mike for a minute, Mr. Crandon climbed the stairs and pounded with his free fist on Katherine Banks's front door.

It took a few minutes before a light moved behind the windows and Katherine called out, "Who is it?"

"Amos Crandon! And I've brought you a runaway scallawag!"

The door flew open, and Katherine—holding a small oil lamp and drawing her dressing gown around her—stepped aside so they could enter. "Mike!" she cried. "What happened?"

"I was trying to find—" he began, but Mr. Crandon interrupted.

"Oh, he'll have some tall stories to tell you, I'm sure, but the fact is that he was running away—trying to cross the river, no doubt." He gave Mike a shove forward and stepped back to the door. "I have no more time to waste with this affair," he said. "The boy is in your hands now, and the sooner you send him back to New York, the better it will be for all of us." He slammed the heavy door as he left.

Mike could feel the tears running down his cheeks. He couldn't make them stop, but he had to explain the truth to Mrs. Banks. "I was so afraid," he said. "I thought that Mr. Friedrich had killed Reuben and buried his body, but he hadn't. When we dug up the place behind the hickory trees, we found only a chest of German coins that Mr. Friedrich had buried."

Katherine moved toward him. "Oh, poor Mike," she said. "Look at you. You're bruised. Your hands are bleeding. Come into the kitchen with me. Here—I'll light another lamp."

But Mike backed away from her. "Please let me finish the telling," he said. "The men called Ned and Tom said they'd come back to Mr. Friedrich's farm with the marshal, and there'd be other places to dig up to search for Reuben's body." He paused and took a deep breath.

"Don't you see, Mrs. Banks? I know now Reuben has gone up the Missouri River. If I find him and bring him back to St. Joe, then no one will suspect Mr. Friedrich. If I can't find Reuben, then I've caused more trouble than I've ever thought of in my whole life."

He paused and said, "That's why Mr. Crandon found me at the river."

Katherine put down her lamp, knelt, and enfolded Mike in her arms, but as she stroked his shoulder he couldn't help crying out from the pain.

She rested back on her heels. "What is it, Mike?"

"My back is a bit sore, that's all," he said.

Her eyes narrowed. "Has someone beaten you?"

When he didn't answer, Katherine said, "Let's take off your coat, Mike. I've got some ointments on hand. Maybe there's one I can put on your back to help you feel better."

Mike took off his coat, and Katherine cried, "There's blood on your shirt!"

She led him into the kitchen and tenderly removed the shirt. With a cool cloth she sponged the raw spots on his skin and lightly rubbed them with some of the ointment. During the process she didn't say a word, but when she had finished and stepped away to wrap Mike in a clean shirt of her own, he could see her eyes glittering with angry tears.

"Now you'll have hot milk, with a spoonful of brown sugar in it," she said. "Then I hope you'll tell me all that has taken place since you went to live with the Friedrichs. And when Andrew comes, we'll tell him, too."

"I don't want to go back to New York and prison," Mike whispered.

"I promise you won't," Katherine said. "Trust me."

So Mike began to tell her all that she wanted to hear. He went on until sleep so slowed his words that they tripped into dreams of a warm bed, a hot wrapped brick for his feet, and Katherine's soothing murmur mingled with a deep voice in the hallway.

When sunlight splashed Mike's face, it took him a few moments to remember where he was. As he sat up in bed, he discovered that the pain in his legs and back wasn't as terrible as it had been. His face flushed in embarrassment, until he remembered that Andrew Mac-Nair had come, and it was he who had removed the rest of Mike's clothes and applied the ointment to his legs.

Clean clothes lay waiting for him on the chest by the bed. Mike quickly dressed and ran down the stairs to the kitchen, where Mrs. Banks was stirring some eggs into a heated pan.

"I heard you up," she said. "Your breakfast will soon be ready."

"Thank you for all that you did for me," Mike said shyly. "And Mr. MacNair ..."

As he glanced to each side, Katherine said, "Andrew is still at his own home, but it's early yet. He'll be here soon, so that he and I can pay a call on the Friedrichs."

"But your store—who will take care of it?"

"I have a fine assistant. He knows what needs to be done."

Mike sat at the table and put his head into his hands. "I have to find Reuben."

Katherine sat beside him and gently ruffled his hair. "Andrew's taken care of that," she said. "He agreed with your idea that Reuben had gone back to the Missouri and, being a flatboatman, would have headed upriver. So Andrew said he would put out word with the other boatmen to get in touch with Reuben."

"Will they find him? Soon? Could they telegraph?"

"There are no telegraph lines to the west of St. Joe, but don't fret. Word of mouth often can be faster than telegraph."

Mike sighed with relief and leaned back in his chair to enjoy the breakfast that Katherine set before him. As he took his last bite, he heard a stomping and wiping of boots outside the back door. The door opened wide, and Andrew MacNair entered the kitchen.

Andrew's warm smile quickly changed to a look of concern. "Mike, I'm sorry about what happened to you. You won't have to go back to the Friedrichs again. Ever."

Mike jumped to his feet, almost knocking over his chair. "But I do have to!"

Andrew frowned. "Mike, you don't understand. No one will make you go back to New York or stay with the Friedrichs. I will not tolerate Hans Friedrich's beating you."

Mike shook his head as his words tumbled out. "I don't want to stay with them. I'll take my chances with some other family—if anyone will have me—but I need to go with you and Katherine to explain. I have to tell Mr. Friedrich that we are going to find Reuben."

Andrew and Katherine gave each other a look. Then Andrew rubbed his chin and said, "Well, in that case— yes, you may go with us."

As Andrew on horseback and Mike and Katherine in her small four-wheeled buggy pulled into the front yard of the Friedrich house, Mr. Friedrich and Gunter came slowly from the barn to meet them.

Mr. Friedrich squinted against the sunlight, then—as his glance fell upon Mike—nodded with satisfaction. "Good," he said. "You have brought him back."

Andrew swung from his horse and looped the reins through the hitching post. "Mike came of his own accord," he said.

"Even better. It shows that discipline is a good master. We will make a law-abiding man of him yet."

143

Gunter's eyes widened, and he blurted out, "Papa! You said you would send Michael back to New York!"

"I spoke those words when I was upset. I have changed my mind. I have an obligation, and I cannot shirk it."

Gunter's face darkened and twisted in anger, and Mike saw him clench his fists. *Wait till you find out that I'll soon be gone, you scheming bucket of tallow!* Mike thought. *Of the two of us, I'll be much the happier to get away from you!*

Andrew, who had tethered the horses, took Katherine's hand as she stepped from the buggy. Mike scrambled down the opposite side.

"May we go inside?" Andrew asked. "There are things which need to be said."

"Of course," Mr. Friedrich answered. He led them through the front door and into the parlor, where Mrs. Friedrich joined them, eyes wide in amazement.

"Oh, Michael!" she cried. For an instant she held her arms out as though she wanted to embrace him. Instead she shot a fearful glance at her husband and meekly folded her hands together at her waist.

"Please sit down," Mr. Friedrich said as he plopped into the largest overstuffed chair. "Irma, tell Marta to bring something to eat and drink."

Katherine raised a hand. "No, please. We won't be here long."

Mike, who stood as the others took seats, tried to ignore Gunter's scowling face and said in one long breath, "Mr. Friedrich, I wanted to tell you why I left your house during the night. I went to the river to try to find news of Reuben Starkey, and to send him word to come back to St. Joe so that people would know he was all right and no one would think badly of you and come to your land to bother you."

"I do not care what people think!" Mr. Friedrich said.

"But I do," Mike said.

Mr. Friedrich looked puzzled and asked, "Why should you care?"

Mike wondered himself why he felt pity for Mr. Friedrich, but he did. "I'm sorry about Ulrich," he said.

"Ulrich! He shamed me!"

"He did the wrong thing—as I did—" Mike said, "because he was trying to feed you."

Mr. Friedrich staggered to his feet and paced to one end of the room and back. "Ulrich was a thief. He liked being a thief! Because he was clever and was not caught, he stole more than we needed. You have seen the money."

Before Mike could answer, Mr. Friedrich shouted, "It was after Ulrich was arrested that I found the money he'd hidden away! What could I do with it? How could I give it back? Ulrich was arrested for petty theft. If I turned in that money, it would have gone harder for him! All these years I've kept it, but I'll have you know, I have never spent a single coin! We've worked for all we have in this country!"

Mrs. Friedrich choked back a sob, and her husband turned to her, holding out the palms of both hands. "How could I know Ulrich would become ill in jail, Irma?"

She wiped her eyes and pleaded with Andrew. "We have always been afraid someone would suspect we had the money and come after us. We began to think Reuben was the one. But we did nothing to harm him. He was sent away, and that is the truth."

"Reuben will be found," Andrew said. "I can promise you that."

Mr. Friedrich fell back into his chair and rubbed one hand over his chin, breathing heavily, until the dark red flush left his face and he could speak calmly again. "Is there anything more that Michael has to tell me?"

"Just—just that I'm—I'm sorry," Mike said.

"Very well, you have said it. Now—there are chores

to be done, and you are wasting time." He frowned at Andrew. "We are all wasting time."

"What I have to say won't take long," Andrew said.

Mike heard Gunter snicker and quickly glanced at him. On Gunter's face was that wicked smile Mike knew meant trouble. Gunter had plans. Well, this time he wouldn't get away with it. Mike was determined to stick close to Mr. MacNair and Mrs. Banks.

Or maybe—this would be Mike's last chance to see Gunter caught. He interrupted Andrew. "I'd like to go out to the barn while you talk with Mr. Friedrich."

"That's probably a good idea," Andrew said.

Mike left the house by the front door, ran down the steps, and quickly ducked to the side, where he squatted and flattened himself against the wall. In just a few moments he heard footsteps clattering down the steps, and he peered out to see Gunter heading around the opposite side of the house.

As soon as Gunter was out of sight, Mike ran back up the steps and slipped into the parlor, seating himself next to Mrs. Banks. Although she gave him a quick, surprised glance, the adults were so deeply into their discussion they paid little attention to Mike.

"You are telling me I don't know how to raise boys?" Mr. Friedrich huffed. "I raise them the way my father raised them, the way I should have raised Ulrich!"

"Boys should not be beaten," Andrew said firmly.

"Beatings are all that boys understand," Mr. Friedrich shouted.

"Obviously we don't agree, Mr. Friedrich," Andrew said. "I can't allow Mike to stay with you. He can gather his own things together, and we'll take him with us to town."

There was a commotion in the kitchen, which Mr. Friedrich ignored. "*Nein!*" he said. "We have an agreement! The committee—"

Just then Gunter slammed down the hallway yelling, "Papa! Come quick! Michael set fire to the privy! I saw him! He set the fire and ran!" By this time he was inside the parlor, gripping the doorframe and wheezing heavily. "I saw—" he managed to get out before he looked directly at Mike.

"How could this be? Michael has been here with us." Mrs. Friedrich gazed at Gunter in astonishment.

For an instant there was a shocked silence. Then Gunter shouted, "I don't want him to live here! I don't need another brother! When Ulrich was alive he was the most important just because he was the first, and Michael—you give him special treats. He—" Gunter stopped suddenly, as though he'd remembered something, and mumbled, "The privy really is on fire."

Everyone ran through the house and out the kitchen door to join Marta, who had already beat out a small blaze at one side of the outhouse where an obvious pile of small sticks and leaves lay.

Mr. Friedrich stared at his son with such misery he looked as though he were fighting back tears.

Mrs. Friedrich pulled out a handkerchief and dabbed at her eyes. "Oh, Michael," she said, "we have been much to blame. Could we have another chance?"

Mike was glad he didn't have to answer, because he liked Mrs. Friedrich. Andrew took Mike's hand and said firmly, "I'm sorry, but I've made the decision. Mike will have a new home. It's better that way."

There were tearful hugs from Mrs. Friedrich and a smiling hug from Marta, who whispered, "Never fear, I'll soon be seeing you again."

Mike turned to give Marta a last wave as Katherine drove the buggy out onto the road to St. Joseph.

He leaned back against the leather seat, watching Mr. MacNair, who rode ahead. Maybe someday he'd be tall and strong, with broad shoulders like Andrew MacNair's and a horse and saddle to call his own, and he'd ride over the countryside with the sun beating on his back. But that was far into the future.

Mike sighed and turned to Katherine. "Andrew said I'd have a new home, but I'm thinking he'll have a hard time finding someone who'll want me."

Katherine smiled. "There's someone who wants you very much, if you're willing."

Mike sat erect. "Who?"

"Remember Captain Joshua Taylor?"

"I could never forget him," Mike said. "He's a fine man."

"He thinks you're a fine person, yourself. I received a letter from him just a few days ago. His wife has joined him, and they wrote to ask if there were any chance you'd be free to come to Fort Leavenworth in Kansas to live with them."

Mike knew he was gaping and gasping like a fish thrown out of water. "Live in a real fort?" he managed to say. "And with Captain Taylor and his wife? Oh! Wouldn't that be grand!"

"Life on an army post might be more difficult than life on a farm or in a town," Katherine said. "We've never placed a child with a family on an army post, and there may be problems we can't foresee."

Mike saw himself flattened along the back of a small, spotted pony, rifle slung over his shoulder, battered hat pulled over his eyes as he raced ahead of a whooping, battle-crazed tribe of Indian renegades. He had to reach the fort. He had been the only one brave enough to carry the message to the wagon train, and now he was the only one who would dare to ...

Mike brought himself out of his daydream to grin at Katherine as the happiness bubbled up inside of him. "Well now," he asked her, "do you think I'd ever in my life let a few problems get the best of me?"

As Grandma closed the journal, Jennifer reached for it. "What happened to Mike when he went to Fort Leavenworth to live? Can you tell us?"

"Of course I can," Grandma said, and tried to look mysterious. "But some of Mike's story comes much later in Frances Mary's journal. I think you should hear about Megan's new family next."

"Megan—was she younger than Mike?" Jeff asked.

"No," Grandma said. "She was twelve—a year younger than Frances and a year older than Mike—but I told you Mike's story before Megan's because he was the one who involved his brothers and sisters on that orphan train journey to the west."

"Wasn't Megan the responsible sister?" Jennifer asked.

Grandma nodded. "Yes. Responsible ... in spite of her fears."

"What fears?" Jennifer leaned forward to listen.

"When Megan was very young she was badly frightened by an old woman who grabbed her hand, read her palm, and cackled that bad luck would be with her all the days of her life. 'A bad penny you are,' the gypsy had said and, unfortunately, Megan believed her."

"What happened to Megan?" Jeff asked. "Did she really have bad luck?"

"It depends upon what you call luck," Grandma said. "Goodness knows some terrifying things happened to Megan."

"What?" Jennifer asked.

"Well, there was the time Megan was trapped by hunger-crazed wolves, and another time when she came face-to-face with an escaping outlaw."

Grandma stood and stretched. "I've got some errands to run in town," she said. "Who wants to go with me?"

"Grandma! Don't stop there!" Jeff groaned and flopped over on the sofa.

149

"When are you going to tell us about Megan?" Jennifer complained. "I mean, you've told us this much and—"

Grandma put a finger over Jennifer's lips and laughed. "Oh, there's much more to Megan's story than you can imagine," she said, "so I'll save it until we have more time. How about tomorrow?"

About the Author

JOAN LOWERY NIXON is the acclaimed author of more than sixty fiction and non-fiction books for children and young adults. She is a three-time winner of the Mystery Writers of America Edgar Award and the recipient of many Children's Choice awards. Her popular books for young adults include the first book in the Orphan Train Quartet, *A Family Apart, The Kidnapping of Christina Lattimore, The Specter,* and *The Seance.* She was moved by the true experiences of the children on the nineteenth-century orphan trains to research and write the Orphan Train Quartet.

Mrs. Nixon and her husband live in Houston, Texas.